ELIXIR

ELIXIR

BY
Camille Sharon

Illustrations by A. R. Meyering
Cover art by Camille Sharon

ISBN 978-1-7360036-0-2

THANKS TO

Kathleen Thien
Katherine Lench-Meyering
A. R. Meyering
Charles Garside

And all the cats over the years

RoRo
Banshee
Pandora
La Purr
Purrcy
Panda
Diva
Oskar
Winky
LuLu
Sushi
Shio
Crichton
Rosie
O'Keefe
Magritte
Karloff
Trapper
Radar
Hot Lips

TABLE OF CONTENTS

CHAPTER 1 - ENGLAND

3 March 1854 (from the personal journal of Diego Amador)

Normally I wouldn't note yet another night of eating alone in the local pub as anything remarkable, but tonight it was not quite like every other night.

First, let me make mention that one of the reasons I don't note my daily eating habits is my frustration with them since moving to London. I understand that it takes time to not only establish my practice, but to also build friendships which elevate the night necessity of feeding myself from a chore to a pleasure. As of yet, I have not built those relationships. In German (and my German is worse than my English) there are two words fressen and essen. They both mean the same thing: to eat. But "essen" is for people and "fressen" is for animals. Since moving to London, I feel like "ich fresse". There is nothing human about it. I eat to stay alive. Not for enjoyment, as it should be. Not to spend time with friends, but because I must.

In my inquiries I have learned of Spanish communities where I would be able to find friendly faces and conversation, but I could have stayed in my homeland if this was enough to sustain me. I'm here, in a foreign land, to experience what it is like to be foreign. To learn the true culture. To swim in it, even if I feel at times as if I am drowning.

And so tonight, like countless nights before, I found myself at the public house down the road. I sat in my familiar corner and adopted my familiar frown which I wear in spite of myself. I don't mean to drive people away with my expression, I just haven't trained myself to wear another one. I haven't even figured out how to make that open "come talk to me" expression which so many Englishmen wear naturally. But tonight, as I sat eating a cold piece of chicken (I must learn to cook or find a better place to eat if I don't make friends soon!) a woman ran in screaming for a doctor.

But now is no time for lies. Calling her a "woman" is generous by any stretch of the imagination. I have seen prostitutes before, and been tempted in my darker hours to visit the less savoury regions of the city which are haunted by these creatures. But to see one in such need like this, it was possible to see past the mask and for a moment to realize that if circumstances were different for her, or for Isabel... But it's best not to dwell on thoughts which can have no effect on present events. I spoke up.

The look in her eyes was heart breaking. She was clearly terrified to be seeking help in the first place, yet driven to it by her desperation. And here I was, her potential salvation. Would I be able to help? She led me away.

Not being in the habit of dining with my satchel, I didn't have any supplies for whatever malady lay before me. I advised the woman that it was necessary to stop first at my residence so I could collect a few things before proceeding to wherever it was that she was leading me. I was not overjoyed to bring such a creature of the night home, even if under such innocent circumstances, but I had little choice since she refused to tell me where I could meet up with her and letting me out of her sight now that she had found me didn't seem likely. Had I been thinking clearer I would have questioned why she was in such close proximity to my own neighbourhood. It isn't the kind of place where one goes to encounter people with nocturnal professions, but I was thinking only of my calling – to treat someone in need.

After packing a few necessary items in my case, off I went with this woman. She told me her name was Pearl, but the veracity of every word out of her mouth needs must be called into question, even something as simple as a name. I was surprised that she only led me a few blocks away from my own home. Again, I shouldn't have been surprised by that except that Pearl was so out of place in this world. A world where I myself struggle to belong. But in hindsight it is completely logical that she would be seeking help nearby and would not have travelled across town from pub to pub looking for a doctor. I was probably in the first place she had looked. Fortune was smiling on her for once in her life and I was that fortune. Perhaps the meeting will ultimately prove to be fortuitous for us both.

The flat Pearl took me to was in a slightly nicer building than my own. The room was spare, as if unlived in. Again, I found myself to be the victim of my own conclusions. I incorrectly assumed that I would be treating Pearl, or a friend of hers, for some illness which plagues people in their "profession." I had made sure to pack as many medicines and preparations I could think of which might help treat that sort of disorder. It was to my surprise that upon arriving at the flat I was shown into the bedroom where a man (well-dressed and well-spoken) sat on the edge of the bed holding a damp, blood-soaked towel against his hand.

This man was much older than Pearl. Much older than myself. His injury was minor in truth. A cut on his hand. He was evasive about how exactly it had happened. He was evasive about every question I had! I got the hint very quickly and went about cleaning the wound and bandaging his hand without any talk. Pearl did her best to remain calm, but she kept peeking her head around the corner to see how we were progressing.

When I finished bandaging the man's hand, he broke the silence. He asked my name and where my office was. He requested (a word which I use euphemistically) that if I speak of treating him, I tell people he showed up at my office just as I was leaving for the day and that I treated him there. He could tell by my confused expression that I didn't understand why I should make a good story out of treating a man's cut hand, and then it dawned on him – I didn't know who he was!

Convinced I would soon enough find out, he took me into his confidence. And by taking me into his confidence I mean he paid me an enormous amount for my services and made some not-so-veiled threats that I go along with the story he was about to tell me or my life wouldn't last long enough to benefit from my newfound fortune. His name was Ian Wilkinson. It had a ring of familiarity to it, but I still could not place it. It seemed that for the first time since coming to London, being an outsider had proved to be an advantage. This man wanted anonymity and he had stumbled into it.

He refused to tell me what really happened, but based on the broken glass in the other room, it wasn't hard to decipher. It wasn't a mystery why he didn't want me to mention the presence of Pearl, but why he wanted me to change the location of the events was a mystery. Wasn't this his apartment?

I was abruptly shown the door once he was satisfied that I had done all I could for him that night. He assured me that he would keep the dressing clean and that I would see him again. He would be coming to see me in a few days so I could check on the progress of his injury. Not really necessary for such a minor abrasion, but part of his cover up.

I know I shouldn't be so eager to learn who this man is, but I must admit that I'm overcome with curiosity and over the coming weeks I will seek out information about this man to learn why his life is so secretive. But no matter what dark realm I've entered, I cannot help but feel intense excitement over the prospect of being regularly acquainted with this man.

3 March 1854

My Dearest Isabel,

What important things we used to speak of as children! I remember many nights when the moonlight was so bright it cast shadows on the walls and your little voice would come floating into my room in a whisper. I would speak endlessly about leaves and bugs I had discovered while you recounted the time spent with mother that day.

I am so pleased that you have decided to continue your language studies and that you are allowing me to take part in your training. With each pen stroke I think to myself what a joy it is to write to you in our "secret language." Now that I'm living in London, I'm surrounded by English, but I'm constantly surprised by how little I understand! The accents here are so diverse and people speak so quickly, I spend most of my time repeating the simple phrase "slower, please" more than I say anything else. I long for those carefree days of childhood when we would slip into our poorly constructed sentences, convinced no one else in the world could understand us. We gave away the secrets of the universe!

Adjusting to life in London has been a challenge, but my practice is starting to pick up. You will note that my address has changed. I finally have a large enough clientele to move out of my one meagre room above the bakery and into an actual flat. I expect that by the end of the year I'll be established well enough that I'll even be able to take a short vacation. Perhaps a visit to you and your new husband in my beloved Andalusia? Nothing would give me greater pleasure than to see my family after what seems like a lifetime away.

Something strange I have noted, to my benefit, is that the people here seem to adore superstitions. Not that they are superstitious, but they are fascinated by things which they think might be magical, and so my darker complexion, something which I thought would scare patients away, actually has helped me gain patients. I'm not just a doctor, I'm a mysterious "gypsy" who they suspect might, in addition to the traditional medical knowledge, possess some skills beyond human understanding to help cure all the faster. Or cure the incurable. I've hung a wonderful exotic tapestry in my front window to add to the atmosphere. The seller didn't know the origin - the thought it perhaps to be African.

Please write soon.

All my love,

Diego

26 March 1854

I paid the first of many similar house calls today. Not the usual kind of house call. There was no frantic husband in the parlour, pacing while a servant woman boiled water, uncertain of what else either of them could do to help. No. Although my practice is relatively new, a business opportunity has arisen that is too good to pass up, and, alas, to take it, I must call on all of my patients and let them know that I will no longer be able to treat them.

It is all happening so quickly! My mind races. For the past week I have been seeking out my fellow followers of Hippocrates to make good matches for all of my patients. I know I could have simply closed up shop and left them to flounder in their ailments, but I feel my obligation to the calling runs deeper than just treating those who come to me in need. I must also monitor their wellbeing when they are in health.

My client list is daunting! I had no idea I had amassed such a following. My days were not all filled to capacity, but most of my patients didn't require regular care, so it is easy, upon reasoned reflection, to comprehend how this list could be so vast.

After identifying the medical practitioners whose work I respected and who I felt comfortable entrusting my clients with, I went about sorting through that client list. I spent countless hours writing letters to a portion of the list – those patients who I knew were only stopping in for a one time visit and who I was unlikely to encounter again. If they needed a doctor again, I was providing them with the name of one. I do have a handful of patients requiring a more personal touch. And so today began my due diligence in making house calls to comfort where a letter would not suffice. In rare cases I will still be able to continue treatment as I transition the patient to their new doctor, but I am not sure how much of my time my new position will occupy and I don't want to be confronted by a situation where I am not able to follow through on my promise of continuing, although lessening, aid.

Felicity sought me out because I was foreign. Poor dear... I didn't really feel I could help her much. She needed someone to talk to more than she needed any kind of medical treatment. She had inherited an enormous amount of money, but she found no happiness in the luxurious life it could provide. She was concerned that everyone she met was trying to steal from her and that all men were only interested in her for the wealth and status which would come from marrying her, not in her own person.

She came to see me at erratic times, always hiding in the doorway across the road, watching for all of my patients to leave, then stealthily entering my office just as I was getting ready to leave for the day. Part of her worry was that everyone in London knew who she was and was plotting to steal from her. Since I was not from London and didn't know anything of the city's politics, I was somehow excluded from her delusion. The only treatment I offered her came in the form of sleeping powders and herbs to help calm her nerves.

I wasn't sure what to expect as I walked up to her home, and I'm still trying to comprehend exactly what I saw. The exterior was in some state of disrepair. There was a masonry gate surrounding the property which had been worn with time and the grass inside the yard was unkempt. Bald in places, overgrown in others. The pavement was cracked as gnarled roots from an overgrown tree pressed at it from underneath. This was not a happy yard where children would play or where Felicity would spend time comforting herself with a spade in her hand. This was a place to be passed through as one travelled to and from the house. Best not to linger.

I rang the bell, and I found myself holding my breath hoping at the same time that she wouldn't invite me inside because I was apprehensive of what I would find there, and hoping out of morbid curiosity that she would invite me inside so I could get a look! She did answer the door and before I could even speak, she took my hand and drew me in. She darted her head out as if to search for unseen followers and then once we were both safely inside, she bolted the door closed and locked it with a key. Like it or not, I was here as long as she wanted me. Luckily, she was a slight creature and would be easy to overpower if it became necessary.

Inside, the property was not in a better state. I hadn't spent much time treating this woman, or perhaps I would have been better prepared to see how she lived. There was barely enough room to walk as she led me from the parlour to the living room. Every surface was piled with papers and books and cloth. The rooms were dim with heavy curtains drawn over the windows, so I could only catch glimpses of all of the assorted items littered everywhere. One table we passed was covered in what looked like jewels! I longed to linger here and examine this unexpected treasure, but I was there with a purpose and I needed to get to it.

A fire blazed in the living room making the cramped room unbearably hot. Felicity didn't seem to notice, but it was necessary in the heat that I remove my coat and hat. Felicity took this as a sign that I intended to settle in and visit for a while. She cleared off a chair, moving the stack of items to the floor, and urged me to sit. I obliged and she disappeared into the kitchen, returning a moment later with a silver tea service.

Before I could begin, Felicity began to talk. Whatever other afflictions she suffered from, her tongue and lungs were not affected. She could talk for hours. I strongly suspect it mattered not if there was another person present to listen to her, for even if there was, she seldom allowed them a moment to get as much as two words out before she started up again.

I sat and listened to her for a very long time before finally being able to seize upon an opportunity. In moments of lucidity it would occur to Felicity that she needed to hear the voice of the other person to actually qualify the discourse as a conversation, so every so often she would invite a reply. "Don't you think so?" or "And what do you have to say on the subject?" or "I mean, you wouldn't say I was wrong, would you?" I navigated my way through several of these. "Oh, no. I don't think so at all." "I quite agree." "You're quite right." Those were the only sorts of answers a person could give before the stream of words once again poured freely from those lovely lips...

And they were lovely. That was part of the problem. Felicity was a beautiful young woman. Men did approach her. She had three marriage proposals before her seventeenth year, yet she didn't think any of the men loved her. At least not for approved of reasons. She mistakenly thought they were after her fortune, but just as often, I'm convinced, they were interested in having a beautiful young wife. All the better if she was rich, but they'd still have had her if she had been destitute.

Eventually the conversation changed. "So, tell me, Diego, what have you been up to?" she asked. Here was my chance. I started to explain my new circumstances to her, how I was helping my patients find new doctors. It seemed to be going well until I mentioned his name.

Ian Wilkinson.

No sooner had the name left my lips than all of the colour left Felicity's face. She stood and silently walked to the door. I repeated what I had already said about how I would still visit her, and then the silence ended.

I had heard her talk about people betraying her. I knew that she was deranged and that the stories she told were figments, yet here I was the victim of one of her delusions. She became irate, yelling at me. She flung the door open and demanded that I leave. Before I could escape, finding the room difficult to navigate in a hurry with all the clutter, I tell her if it was Ian who had been paying me all along to spy on her. My protests fell on deaf ears and her rant became less coherent. She closed the door again and turned on me, a murderous look in her eyes. She ran off a list of names asking if each was the person secretly employing me. She insisted that I would never have her money.

Somehow, although Lord help me, I'm not sure now exactly what I said, I managed to calm her enough to open the door again and let me outside. Once I was outside, I turned back toward her to try and reason with her and explain that I still wanted to help her, if I could. She threw something at my head and threatened to call the constable if I didn't leave immediately.

Having realized that I was not immune to her insanity, as I had previously been naïve enough to believe, I began to feel grave concern for her future as I walked home. If she did not find someone to connect with, to trust soon, she would find herself in the asylum. Her wealth, her youth, her beauty, these things had kept her safe for this long, but people are not as tolerant of someone who is weathered as they are of someone who has not yet begun to show the ravages of time.

I will keep seeing her, even if at each visit she greets me with malicious glares. My conviction to help her is stronger than ever now. There must be some way to calm her mind, to calm her spirit.

The visit from today, although not nearly as long as I had anticipated or planned, has left me exhausted. I feel as though my own vital force has been drained from me, something I would willingly have shared with Felicity if it seemed to do any good. Instead I'm exhausted, unable to continue working today and in dire need of rest, and Felicity is none the better.

I'll set out again tomorrow, earlier, to see more of my patients, make more house calls. The others shouldn't be as challenging as they all suffer from much easier to diagnose and therefore easier to treat ailments. In my restful hours I will have to devote some time to devising a plan for Felicity's treatment which will have better success than what we have had thus far.

27 March 1854

Querido Diego,

It is always such a treat to receive one of your letters! I am so pleased to hear that your business is going well. And I do so envy you living in London! Would that I could come visit you instead of our discourse leading us in the opposite direction, but I have news of my own which makes it impossible for me and Antonio to contemplate traveling for the foreseeable future – I am with child.

What apprehension I feel when I know I should be overjoyed. Married life, although I can hardly be considered an expert at it, has not been everything I imagined it would. While I do care deeply for Antonio, I suppose I imagined things would be different than they actually are. I long to roam the world! There is so much I haven't seen! So much to learn and taste and touch and experience! And yet, I may never get the chance. My life now belongs to Antonio and soon to our child.

His parents live very close by, which is something else for which I wasn't prepared. I thought when I left home that I was done being mothered. That I would finally get to take charge of my own life, at least in part, but instead I not only must consider Antonio's needs but his mother seems to always be at our home. I can't even make the decision of what we will eat for dinner without first consulting her. She goes with me when I do the shopping. She watches me as I clean. When I sit and read, she asks me what I'm doing. I suppose I should consider this as practice for when I am a mother myself – the patience I need to deal with her I'll need with my own child.

I have asked Antonio if we couldn't leave here, but he loves it too much to even entertain the idea. Each day I struggle to resign myself to my situation. By the end of each day I've gotten through another, though, and eventually I'm certain the days will all be easy to get through.

Our own mother doesn't visit as much as I would like, but Father can't travel easily any longer and even though the journey isn't far, she doesn't like to make it without him, leaving him on his own. She does ask about you. I know that isn't a topic you want to discuss, but she hopes you are well.

Please write often.

Besos,

Isabel

3 April 1854

I finished packing the trunks today and will make my journey to the countryside tomorrow. As I sit in my empty flat, I am struck by several things. Firstly, I have no true happy memories here. It has been a pleasant place to live, in a nice building with friendly enough neighbours, but no sense of community. I have not once been invited over to dinner. In Spain, as a single doctor, the dinner invitations were endless. Secondly, I have actually begun to amass quite a sizable collection of possessions, which must mean that I am at my very core allowing London to be my home. I moved out here with just one case, and now I'm not even sure how I'll transport everything to my new home. As I packed up, I thought of what it would be like if I were to move back to Spain, which of these items I would take, which I would sell or give away, and I decided that I didn't want to give anything away, even if there was no way to transport it. Having these things is currently important to me. It makes London seem like home. It ties me to this place and for the first time in my life, I want to be tied to a place.

At once I am overcome with anticipation at starting yet another new chapter of my life (they have been coming so quickly since moving!) and some sadness at having to let the current chapter close. But if I do not let this current chapter close, my life will stagnate. I must step boldly into my new life and embrace the new experiences and new opportunities which life affords me.

**

Before boarding the train for the country, I decided to make one last house call. Mary and Thomas Highgate came to see me out of desperation. They had visited many physicians because after many blissful years together, they could not conceive. They hoped that there was more magic than medicine about me. I was sorry to disappoint them. I don't know why I felt like seeing them, we only had the one visit, but I felt a compulsion to go see them and let them know that even though I was no longer accessible to them, if I ever heard of any magic which could help them, I would let them know. They seemed pleased that I took the time to visit – that I even remembered them.

Now I sit on the train, speeding through the country toward my new life. What adventures lay before me?

3 April 1854

My Dearest Isabel,

Before you mistakenly think you are reading an old letter, let me first say how pleased I am to hear that you will soon have an addition to your family! Overjoyed! Your letter arrived just in time to catch me today before I left my flat for my new home.

Yes! This is why I showed concern that you might believe you had read this before. I am moving yet again! I know it is fast, but so much has happened since I wrote to you last.

I had a mysterious encounter with a man named Ian Wilkinson which has led to a remarkable new opportunity. We met by chance when he needed some help one night and since that time, he has been to see me regularly to treat his own minor injuries, but also with a stream of people who he looks after. After several weeks of nearly daily visits he asked me to be his personal physician. I'm sitting on a train at this moment as I write to you, heading out to his country estate where he lives with his extended family, to become his newest staff.

Though this is not something I had ever envisioned for myself, Lord Wilkinson is influential in political circles and being taken into his household will improve my social standing immensely. I will travel with him when his business requires he be away from home, even if only to London (although he travels throughout Europe with some frequency), and I will be based in a private cottage on his estate.

He has given me the freedom to consult with some of my established patients when we travel to London, so I haven't had to give up my practice entirely, although I am preparing for the inevitability of this event.

The other wonderful part of my taking this job is that I will be able to see you without question now! I have already discussed my plans to visit you, my dear sister, and he wholeheartedly supports me in this. He even mentioned the possibility of his business travels taking him to Spain. If that happens, I'll be able to see you even sooner than we are planning.

Writing to you now helps stave off my impatience at the long ride. I cannot arrive at my new home soon enough.

How different our lives have become. I don't know how you must feel now so tied to Andalusia, but I can only imagine that once I find a woman to love I will be happy to live anywhere so long as she is there. Even if we live in a hovel in a foreign land where neither of us know the language or the culture, I believe we would draw strength from each other and our lives would be as rich as if we were royalty. What the fool I must sound. It is easy for me to idly imagine what married life will be like and vastly different for you living it.

My travels so far have not taken me very far, so please don't envy them. Being alone, eating alone... London is a city rich is culture and art, but the glory is not as grand when you have no one to share it with. I have seen much and hope to see even more in my new position, but for all the world I might drink in I am still hollow inside.

But it is time for us both to focus on our happy futures! The anticipation of reaching my destination has my pulse racing as if I'd run frantic through the streets, yet all I do is sit here and look out the window at the changing scenery. In sleep perhaps my frenetic mind will find some peace.

Stay strong, sister. Antonio loves you and I'm sure his only thought is to make you happy.

All my love,

Diego

5 April 1854

Is it possible that so quickly I have been struck by Cupid's arrow? Grace. Grace! I want to write her name a thousand times and scream it to the mountains! I get ahead of myself, I know, but never have I been so overtaken, so intoxicated by another human being as I have been by Grace!

I knew Lord Wilkinson had a large family, else why would he need a private physician? Yet I never imagined that his family would include the most beautiful, gentle creature on Earth.

I did consider that when I first laid eyes upon her I was still delirious from my travels, in dire need of food and rest. But even after a good night's sleep and the wonderful cooking of the Wilkinson's kitchen staff, I swooned when Grace came into the room. Is this how Isabel felt when she first met Antonio? She's never mentioned it. I'll have to ask her.

I have only had the briefest of encounters with her thus far. She always seems to be rushing off here or there, giddy and free, not burdened by the need to do anything other than be lovely and charming. I have asked Lord Wilkinson if I will have the chance to meet his entire family more formally and he assures me that I will, that it won't be catch as catch can encounters until someone needs assistance, so I must take his word for it that something more formal has been planned to introduce me. I only hope that fair Grace doesn't make another engagement at the same time so that I might have the chance to get to know her better right away. My impatience is nearly unbearable and I fear that if I don't get properly introduced to her soon, I'll do something foolish and improper.

7 April 1854

I am quickly learning the routine and my place in this household. While I am not a servant in the traditional sense, my place is certainly not with the family. I dine in the kitchen with the staff. Or, if I desire, I can take food to my cottage and prepare it in solitude.

The cottage is larger than either flat I was able to afford in London. It has a stove so I am able to keep the dwelling warm and to cook at my leisure. The Wilkinsons' charwoman has informed me that she will perform basic duties in my cottage, although she will not visit daily so I will need to learn to make do. This will be easy for me as I have lived a bachelor's life for some time and have grown accustomed to looking after my own needs.

I am not entirely on the same level as the cook and charwoman. Lord Wilkinson has made me his confidant. I live behind the scenes, but after the house has awakened, I step out of the kitchen and join the family, or at least their patriarch, in the bright halls of the estate. Lord Wilkinson spends most of his day in his study working. He stops occasionally and seeks me out for walks in the country and conversation. So far, the conversation hasn't strayed from the mundane details of his life and the household, but I get the feeling that with time I will learn this man's secrets.

On one of our walks today through his rose garden, which currently houses thorny twigs, I caught a glimpse of Grace! She was wearing the most delicate blue frock, with ribbons in her long golden hair. She carried some early-blooming tulips, freshly picked from the garden. Although there was no wind, her dress and hair seemed to flow as if some otherworldly spirit created a breeze just for her. The dappled sunlight shone on her through the new growth foliage on the trees.

Lord Wilkinson assures me that he will have a formal dinner with his whole family, to which I will be invited, very soon. He is just waiting for his son to return from a short vacation in France, and once the family is complete, I will be introduced to them all at once.

As far as my professional skills, so far, I have only treated the staff. I have been seeing them one by one and treating minor ailments they have been ignoring. I removed a boil from the cook's backside and dressed a small, recent cut on the hand of the stableman. I gave physical inspections to the staff to ensure they were healthy and made general inquiries as to their wellbeing. I suspect once the family has all arrived, I'll perform similar inspections of them, although I do get the feeling that this is not the entire scope of my new position.

10 April 1854

Lord Wilkinson has been called to London unexpectedly for business, so here we are in the same flat where we first met. He has a larger property in the city, but since he only stays for short visits, he keeps this flat out of convenience of not having to worry about the larger house. When he comes for longer visits with his family, that's where they stay, but for now, the flat is where we have settled.

I've only lived in the country for a few days, but already London feels foreign to me. The countryside has always been my home and it feels natural to return to it. The city, now that I see it again, is cramped and dusty. Or perhaps I'm trying to justify to myself that I've made the proper life choice.

Everywhere we go, people look at Lord Wilkinson with recognition. Some people look on with admiration, others with looks worthy of sewer rats. An interesting man surely that I have found myself mixed up with. He has advised me that I am to go with him to his last appointment tomorrow, but I'll be free the first part of the day.

I shall take the opportunity of being back in town to go and visit Felicity tomorrow, if she'll see me. While in London I shall attempt to procure some art supplies. When I was much younger, I would sketch and now I have found a subject which I yearn to draw. The elegant line of her cheek, her hair in ringlets, the flawless skin, the elegant smile.

11 April 1854

The truth has been revealed at last! Not that I didn't suspect, but it is a relief to have it out, in the open. Or at least a shared secret between the two of us. But first let me recapitulate the events of the day.

I started off by visiting Felicity as I had planned. She refused to open the door to me. I have spent some time contemplating her troubles and now that I have felt the powerful effect of Cupid's arrow, I wonder if love might be the remedy she needs to calm her troubled mind. I'm unsure of how to help her in this difficult quest, but if I encounter anything in my travels which might make her heart more receptive to love, or if I find a man who might be up to the challenge of taming this wild creature, I will make it my duty to improve her life by exposing her to the wonders of love. I hope that through persistence she will come to once again trust me so that my council will not fall on deaf ears in these matters. Alas, for this visit, a closed door is all that greeted me and I must console myself with my new resolve to introduce love into this poor creature's life.

Since my visit to Felicity's home was briefer than I had intended, I was able to roam the city and procure some fine charcoal sticks and sketch papers. I'm afraid my skills have lessened for years of neglect, so before I dare even approach the fair Grace and ask her to sit for me. I'll need to spend some hours in diligent practice so that my skills will not disappoint. But already I am elated to begin this new hobby so that I might be able to spend some time with Grace.

I visited my old office and flat, just to see them, although after such a short time away I don't know what I expected. No one new has taken up residence at either location, so they look just as they did when I left.

I didn't have much else to do while waiting for my afternoon appointment with Lord Wilkinson so I returned to the flat early and waited. Lord Wilkinson returned only slightly before our pre-appointed time and we sat and talked. It was then that he revealed all to me.

True, I was hired to be his personal physician and to attend to his family when we were at his estate. On his travels, his health concerns were of a much more private kind. The woman I had met before, Pearl, was his mistress. One of many. In London she was the only one, but in Paris there was another, and another in Frankfurt and another in Madrid. In other cities that he travelled to he didn't keep mistresses, preferring take his chances with what the market had to offer. But as a family man, he didn't want to risk his wife's health by giving in to a night of lustful passion with a filthy whore. He decided for the sake of all to hire a doctor and have all of his women fully inspected, just like one would inspect a piece of livestock prior to purchase. I was to inspect any woman he presented to me and deem her either worthy of his currency, or not.

Have I made a deal with the devil? What kind of power does this man have that he can keep this mistress in the city, under the nose of his wife? Based on the reaction of Felicity, I would imagine that his reputation is not all political, that rumours of his nocturnal activities have spread despite his efforts to silence them. Now I am an unwitting confidante in perversion just as I am seeking to become a respectable man myself. It is only now with some reflection that I can chastise myself for not reacting at the time. I did nothing. I was dumbstruck by these revelations and as Pearl arrived, I did my duty and gave her a full physical examination. "Let me check your teeth, my dear!" Oh, did she realize that by complying with this seemingly innocent request of her benefactor she was dehumanizing herself further in both of our eyes?

Once my inspection was completed and I passed judgment on the female as healthy enough for Lord Wilkinson's needs, I was further repulsed when Lord Wilkinson suggested that I needn't leave the apartment while he and Pearl completed their business, but I had enough of my senses about me to take my leave. He gave me a time frame after which I was expected to return so that we might go to dine together. Tomorrow we leave London, Wilkinson having completed all of the business he came here for, so we would retire early.

I roamed the streets aimlessly for some time trying to gather my thoughts. My feet began to ache from the walking, for my pace quickened as I walked as if all my frustration was being channelled through my legs and feet. My hands, I noticed, were clenched, and even though I would unclench them, as soon as I diverted my thoughts away from my hands they would clench themselves again.

By the time I returned to the flat, Pearl was gone and Wilkinson was cleaning himself up, getting ready for us to depart together for dinner.

I don't recall our dinner conversation. I know I did my best to not reveal my true feelings over what had taken place that day. I have given up so much for this man. There is so much to gain from continuing my association with him. Is keeping his secret that terrible when weighed against the good he has to offer? The travel, the knowledge to be gained in foreign lands... If I betray Wilkinson's confidence, I have much to lose. There is no doubt he is a powerful man and his influence extends beyond the boundaries of this island nation. A betrayal could have dire consequences for my career, for my family, and a betrayal would ensure that I would never see my beloved Grace again.

My only choice is to continue in Wilkinson's employ and hope he has not noticed my distain for his secret, or that if he noticed, he doesn't care.

14 April 1854

David. I sneer when I say it. I can't help myself. My eyes become mere slits and I bare my teeth like a wild animal defending a freshly killed carcass.

As soon as she spoke his name, I felt myself flush. My heart sank deep within my chest and my pulse started racing. I was caged, trapped, yet no one else could see the cage. Even now I feel my pulse quicken as I recollect the events.

The meal was outstanding. We ate golden plover as our main course. I am certain Isabel will want this recipe. I'll have to consult with the cook tomorrow and see if I can convince her to share her cooking secrets with me so that I might in turn share them with my sister. After such a long wait to finally be introduced formally to the entire Wilkinson family it was a grand evening indeed.

Wilkinson's youngest, Rosemary, though only 14, is well on her way to being equally as beautiful as Grace. Her hair is several shades lighter, almost white, and she has allowed it to grow very long, beyond her waist. Robert, their older brother, returned from France while Wilkinson and I were in London. He is a strong young man, ready to take on the world. I fear, however, that he allows the comfort of a wealthy family influence his ambitions.

I must say that I felt some sadness to see Lady Wilkinson at dinner. Knowing that her husband is not faithful to her and seeing how much she loves him and dotes on him did not seem proper. I wonder if it is possible for Wilkinson to love his wife despite his infidelities? Perhaps I'll be able to pose this question to him some day.

Despite our formal introduction, Grace seemed less interested in talking to me than to her sister and mother, with her conversation always returning to the same subject. David. Perhaps I shouldn't react so strongly. It was clear from the way Grace spoke about this David that she doesn't know him well. He is a cousin of a friend of hers who is coming to the country for an extended visit. They met when they were younger. Haven't seen each other in years, she fancied him long ago. Perhaps she'll find him tedious now and I'll have gone through all of this worry for naught.

I have begun my secret art training. I've brought various objects from the house into my cottage to arrange as still life displays to practice sketching. I've decided to start with simple shapes, inanimate objects, and then move onto organic still lifes.

Wilkinson has informed me that we are to depart in a few days for an extended trip to the north of Africa. I look forward to the trip, but leaving Grace at this critical time distresses me.

15 April 1854

My Dearest Isabel,

I am writing to alert you to my imminent travel plans as I do not want you to be alarmed if it takes me a long time to respond to your next letter. I depart tomorrow for an extended tour of North Africa with my employer. I will do my best to write to you and tell you of all the wonders we encounter.

I have finally been introduced to the Wilkinson family. We had a formal dinner last night where I was able to meet the immediate family. There are several extended family members who Lord Wilkinson has informed me will come and go throughout the year – the house is certainly large enough for four times the number of people as were in attendance last night. Once the weather turns slightly warmer the Wilkinson country estate should become quite active with visitors.

I've enclosed a card with the recipe for last night's meal on it so that you might recreate it for Antonio and his family. It took a fair amount of coaxing to get this from the cook! I fear that I now owe a favour in return. But that you might enjoy this meal as I did it will be worth whatever small torment is thrust upon me! I'm not sure you will be able to collect all of the necessary ingredients as several of them are seasonal and regional to this part of England, but I'm sure you have an imagination which is more than capable of finding adequate substitutions.

I hope you are feeling well and that your pregnancy is easy. I am sorry that my trip will further delay our plans for a visit. Honestly, I don't even know how long I will be away! Lord Wilkinson is a mysterious man and there is still much I do not know of him.

This should please you, as you have always been so supportive of my artistic abilities. I have decided to return to my studies in art and have begun to draw again. My first attempts were wobbly messes, but each time I put charcoal to paper I gain confidence. The line appears no longer lost but pushed across the page with intent. If I do find myself getting discouraged, I hear your voice in my ear urging me on to keep at it. You always believed in me and I carry your encouragement with me still.

Be well. I'll look forward to a stack of letters from you on my return so that I can catch up on all your happy news.

Love,

Diego

CHAPTER 2 - AFRICA

17 April 1854 (Diego's Diary)

My first priority when we land in Tangiers will be to query the locals if they have any remedies for seasickness! Three more days aboard this steamer seems unbearable. I keep thinking back to my mother's own folk remedies. How I long for a mint leaf right now! The efficacy of her methods has never been proven, but mint, as I recall, cured a plethora of ills and I could do worse than chew on some now.

I look at Wilkinson as we talk about our pending arrival and I don't see wonder in his eyes. He has travelled too far, seen too much of the world, to still find wonder in it. How tragic that this fate could befall any man. I must make every effort to not let this happen to me. Cynicism can be infectious, and I am afraid I haven't found a remedy for that yet, either.

Wilkinson has asked me to take on another role during our travels – that of interpreter. He was pleased to learn that I had studied not only English but French and Italian as well. He has decided that this means I have an ear for language and that I'll be able to learn the language of the land no matter where we travel! What a strange man. I can only imagine he hasn't heard the word "no" often or he might have realized what an absurd leap this is. Still, he's given me the task to find other passengers who speak Arabic and convince them to teach me enough to get by. I can only imagine that Wilkinson has some adventures planned for us.

I was able to find a young man, Murtaza, only a few years my junior, who has been in London studying. He is returning home now and he has agreed to spend some time on the journey teaching me some basics. Will I be able to learn a whole language in such a short time? La.

A benefit to my new side task is that I am freed from spending all of my time with Wilkinson. He has no interest in learning and he does not appear to respect Murtaza, so when Murtaza is around, Wilkinson manages to find other ways to entertain himself. Despite Wilkinson's feelings, though, I will propose to him that hiring Murtaza as a guide would help ensure us having a successful journey. I have broached the subject with Murtaza and he seems interested in the prospect.

21 April 1854

Since arriving in Tangiers my life has seemed like a parade of girls. I say "girls" because some of them are scarcely older than Rosemary! I must have poked and prodded at least fifteen of the pitiful creatures before finding one which was in good enough health to allow Wilkinson to put her tenuous physical and mental states at risk. Not only did I inspect these girls, but I also have felt it necessary to provide them with treatment and guidance. Heaven only knows why, since their rejuvenation simply makes them more eligible candidates for Wilkinson and those of his ilk.

I do not know where Wilkinson finds these girls. Thankfully, my job thus far has been to remain in our rented apartment for the girls to be brought to me. I feared the whole way over that we would go roaming the streets together to search for these poor souls and that I would have to examine them in dark alleys or bars or brothels or gutters.

After I found the one acceptable girl from the many I examined today, I was free to roam the city for several hours, agreeing to meet up with Wilkinson for a late supper. Murtaza's services as a guide have not yet been required by Wilkinson, but I engaged him for the afternoon to take me around Tangiers. It is an interesting city. Such a mixture of cultures. It is filled with debauchery and danger, yet many other European businessmen like Wilkinson can be found roaming the narrow dusty streets.

We went to the open-air market and I witnessed a unique cultural event: a snake charmer. He attracted a crowd by playing an instrument like a flute, but one I've never seen before, then he opened the top of a basket and a snake, which Murtaza told me was a cobra, did an undulating dance to the music, lifting itself out of the basket. The snake charmer wagered with the people in the crowd that they touch his snake, but no one would accept the challenge. He then wagered that he could kiss the snake on the head, and a few people did take this wager. Well, it was quite the spectacle! While the snake charmer worked, Murtaza explained to me that the cobra is not only deadly if it bites you, but that it also has the ability to spray its venom, making it dangerous for the snake charmer to stand in such close proximity to the beast. Murtaza also cautioned me that it was not a good wager to bet against the snake charmer, though. My curiosity piqued, I've asked him to get me a personal audience with the snake charmer so that I might learn some of his secrets. Murtaza is working on it.

The market is filled with all sorts of oddities. The stalls are lined with dried lizards and snakes and scorpions. All said to have various magical and medicinal properties. I have decided to investigate these local wonders. Perhaps I can find something to help Mary and Thomas and Felicity.

22 April 1854

My Dearest Isabel,

What a mysterious land I am in! You should see the people and the architecture. It is so different from Andalusia. Older. Ancient! The city is a mix of old and new, anachronistic, yet it all feels right somehow.

I went to an open-air market yesterday and saw so many wonderful oddities. I plan to return there as soon as possible to procure an assortment of items unique to the region which are purported to have medicinal qualities. Many of the market stalls have dried reptiles which I fear I may never encounter again.

You will be pleased to know that I am continuing my drawing practice while here, using my sketchpad to help preserve the memories of this place. I have only done one sketch thus far, but I intend to sketch during all of my travels and one day show you my book and tell you in person about all of the wondrous places I have seen!

Today my guide, Murtaza, took me to the outskirts of the city where he introduced me to the local doctor. Everything I was rumoured to be in London, I believe this man was! His medicinal skills were not restricted to science. He had a vast knowledge of folklore and in his home I saw many of the items I had seen for sale in the market the day before.

But I have not told you about Murtaza. I met him on the ship and we formed a fast friendship. It is a relief to have someone else to talk to besides my employer, and while Lord Wilkinson attends to his business and I have free time, Murtaza has agreed to show me what he knows of the city. His city. I agreed to pay him, although the rate we have agreed upon is meagre. I sense that Murtaza is happy to have me to take around as much as I am to be led. And we agreed that if Lord Wilkinson needs a guide at all while here, Murtaza would have the first consideration for the position. Working for Lord Wilkinson would be most lucrative, indeed.

This doctor we visited, Saïd, allowed us to stay with him the whole afternoon. I was able to witness as he treated several patients. He even allowed me to consult on one patient who came in with a cut hand. I supposed he thought that no matter how unskilled I was as a doctor, I would be able to perform a simple wound binding. But with the others, I was only permitted to watch.

His treatments involved ritualistic elements. Dancing and chanting. He would mix combinations of herbs in a mortar and pestle and then, depending on the treatment, either blow the powder in the patient's face, sprinkle it on the ground without ever even having it touch the patient, or he would present it to them, wrapped in a makeshift paper container, with instructions to brew it into a tea when they got home. If I used the ingredients Saïd did, I would have prepared the powder out of sight of my patient! Can you imagine how enthusiastically you would brew a tea which contained powdered snake eyes, regardless of the severity of your ailment?

Between patients, Saïd told us some a local folktale, explaining the various believed medical properties of some of the unusual ingredients we had seen him prescribing to his patients. Here is the story of the chameleon.

A very long time ago, there was a war going on. People did their best to live in peace in their villages, but the soldiers didn't always keep their fights on the battlefield and would sometimes wander into these villages. In one such place, there was a Mother and her Baby. The Father was off fighting, so they were doing the best they could supporting each other. One day, soldiers from the opposing side in the battle came to their city and decided that they should kill or imprison all of the women and children who had been left behind, to demoralize their foes. The Mother prayed to the gods that she and her Baby might somehow survive the onslaught.

The gods did not hear her over the screams of the other villagers, but there was a chameleon in her home who did hear her cries and he decided that he might be able to help them. The chameleon climbed through and open window and spoke to the Mother. "I can help you escape from the soldiers, if you will grant me a favour." Mother was afraid, but she wanted more than anything to protect Baby and would do anything, even listen to a chameleon, if there was a chance of surviving. Without waiting to hear what the chameleon wanted in return, Mother agreed to accept his help.

"Quick, grab only what you need and hold your child close to you."
Mother put on her cloak and picked up Baby, "What now, chameleon?"
she asked.

"Put me on your shoulder," he answered, and Mother did as instructed.
Chameleon was used to disguising his own appearance to hide from
predators, and even though he had never attempted to conceal
something other than himself, or something so large, he was confident
he could. He concentrated very hard, and all at once Mother, Baby and
chameleon seemed to disappear into the background.

Chameleon, who was sitting on Mother's shoulder, whispered in her ear,
"You must leave this place slowly, now, and not make a sound. If you
travel slowly, I can continue to hide you from the soldiers' eyes, but I
have not the skill to conceal you from their perceptive ears. And if you
move too quickly, they are sure to hear you."

Since the soldiers had not yet arrived at Mother's house, she quickly got
to the door, then moved as slow as she could outside. Once outside, she
stayed close to walls and in shadows, to make Chameleon's job easier.
But as she started to gain some distance from the city, she remembered
that she would owe this creature a favour in return, and she was
hesitant to pay. Chameleon, sensing Mother's change of mood,
whispered in her ear again, "My request is simple, so I caution you
against doing anything rash. And, I must warn you, if you discard me
before I have removed your camouflage, you will be forced to roam the
earth this way, you and your child, nearly invisible to all, including each
other."

Mother begged Chameleon to undo his magic from them, but he would
not until they were safely away. Still thinking of Baby, Mother
persevered and got far away from her village, which she could see in the
distance now in flames, burned by the enemy soldiers.

Once safe, the honourable chameleon returned Mother and Baby to
normal and hopped onto a nearby tree. "Madam, the life of a creature in
the wild is difficult. Snakes and birds come after me every day just like
those soldiers came after you. If I had a place to live, with humans, I
would be safe. My desire is the same as yours: safety."

Mother agreed to keep Chameleon with her and Baby, as mutual
protectors.

And this is why the chameleon's skin is believed to cure all kinds of skin
ailments, but primarily rashes and other blemishes, seemingly making
them disappear. And, for those who believe that even deeper magic is
possible, the chameleon's skin is said to bestow invisibility.

Over time, the Baby grew up and became a Man. Chameleon remained his friend through his whole life and when it was time for him to go off and join the war, Chameleon looked around and decided he would go with him. "You and your mother have protected me better than I imagined. I have lived a good life. I had a family. My children grew and left home. You have kept us safe and now that my life is nearing its end, I feel there is no other choice than to go with you to war and do what I can to keep you safe."

Man was pleased that Chameleon wanted to go with him and agreed.

Having Chameleon sitting on his shoulder during battles proved to be a bigger asset than Man had ever dreamed it would be. Not only did Chameleon keep Man safe from attack by hiding him from his enemies' eyes, but Chameleon could also look in a different direction than he faced, so while Man faced the attacker on one side, Chameleon whispered in his ear the positions of potential attackers from all sides.

Stories of Man's skill in battle spread and he soon became feared by the enemy. If they suspected Man was in the approaching war party, they would immediately surrender because they knew they did not have the skills to kill this Man who could hide from their arrows and always knew of their attacks so that no one could take him by surprise.

Because of Chameleon's help, Man was able to bring about the end of the war, becoming a great leader to all because he never misused Chameleon's skill to hurt those who were not attacking, only to defend himself and his side in the battle as honourably as possible.

One evening, after the war, Man sat with Chameleon on his shoulder as he so often had over the years. He noticed that Chameleon was tired and asked him if there was anything he could do. Chameleon answered, "No. I have lived with mankind most of my life. Now I think it is finally time for me to set out on my own and greet the end of my life like a beast."

Man lowered chameleon off of his shoulder and set him on the ground, and they thanked each other for the time they had spent together. As Chameleon walked away from Man, he made himself invisible so that the man could not follow, and because of the special design of the chameleon's feet, he left no tracks to indicate which way he had gone.

It is because of Chameleon's ability to look behind while facing forward that its eyes are used in preparations for eye ailments, to improve eyesight and are thought to bestow special insight in meditation, being rumoured to even provide glimpses of the future. The chameleon's feet are used in bad magic against enemies to hide their own tracks so that they might lose their way and forget where they have been and where they are going.

This is the story Saïd told us today. Perhaps you will save my letters and tell them to my niece or nephew one day. I'll leave that up to you! Or perhaps, with your permission, when I come to visit, I will reminisce fondly of my time in Africa and will tell him the stories myself.

It has been interesting, and I am learning so much.

I also want to say, dearest sister, that knowing I am able to write to you provides me with great comfort.

All my love,

Diego

23 April 1854

Today Murtaza took me to see the snake charmer.

The cobras are kept in deplorable conditions, not that they should be expected to be kept as pets in luxury, but it is surprising that they survive long enough to perform in the charmers' shows the way they are treated. But, as the stranger, a foreigner (a role I have grown accustomed to), I held my tongue on the matter.

The charmer showed me first all of the scars on his own body from his tangles with cobras over his lifetime. How lucky he was to be alive. But he also had built up a tolerance to the venom and had very little fear when dealing with the serpents.

His business went beyond stealing money from tourists, however. He would wander into the desert to capture his own snakes – a commodity of which there was no shortage, so if his own snakes died his loss was only over losing a particularly attractive snake and not that he wouldn't be able to get a replacement within a day. One use for his collection of snakes was to collect the venom from the snakes. Since I am a doctor, Murtaza convinced the charmer to show me how he would milk the cobras, collecting vials of their venom which he sold to scientists for study and to criminals as a highly toxic poison. He did not discriminate in his clientele. He even allowed me to take over milking one of the cobras he claimed was docile, although I'm not sure such a term could ever be ascribed to a wild creature such as this!

He might also be persuaded to sell a snake, never asking questions as to why someone might want to buy it.

The charmer showed off his snakes, even though I wasn't paying, which surprised me. He teased one cobra until it spat at him. Played his instrument and showed me how the snakes moved out of the basket when he did.

But for all this, the most distasteful part of his profession was the deception with the snake which he would take into town with him to show to the tourists. After milking, he explained, once the snake was low on venom and exhausted from struggling against human hands, the snake's jaw could be carefully sewn closed so that during the part of his act where he challenges a spectator to come and participate with the snake it is truly safe for all involved, except for the snake. Unable to eat, unable to drink, it was only able to flick its tongue out to frighten away the timid. Some snakes he would cut the thread off once they had performed a certain number of shows, if they survived, but others would get infections in their skin from the thread and needle passing through their flesh and would turn septic long before hunger or thirst had the chance to claim their lives.

But like I said, this was a commodity of which there was no shortage. The charmer could always get a new snake. He had his show. He had his side business of sales. And dead snakes could also be sold for their food, skin, or to doctors like Saïd for their various magical medicinal purposes.

I was rightly warned not to participate in his show if I saw him in town, as waking up with a cobra in your bed was never pleasant, but if I saw a different charmer and wanted to discredit him, well, this charmer didn't have a problem with that. I asked if all snake charmers in the city bound their snakes with thread so they could not strike, but this charmer refused to confirm this.

26 April 1854

This morning Wilkinson engaged Murtaza's services and the two of them left very early. I believe this is an indication that Wilkinson is finally undertaking the business which has brought us here to Africa. This is much to my relief as I was beginning to wonder if "business" was only pretence for leaving England.

Having the day to myself, with no guide, I stayed close to our apartment. Murtaza had warned me off of certain areas of town, but I was not feeling adventurous today and it was good to have some solitude.

I hadn't realized how much I would prize the quiet times by myself. Having spent so much of my life on my own, trying to make my own name, I always assumed that I was missing vital companionship which would one day be provided by my wife. Wilkinson certainly is not a wife, but the constant companionship we have had since embarking on this trip has given me some small taste of living with someone and I can only hope, that once I'm married, it will be more pleasant with a different person. I hope that the reason I left home, the reason I felt so desperately that I needed to get away, was not because I am not fit to live with another human being, but because of the company to which I have been subjected.

I have doubts even as I write this, because my mind is drawn to Grace. Lovely Grace. I cannot imagine that I would ever tire of looking at her face, of hearing her voice. If we were to spend every moment together from now until the end of time, I do not believe I would find any tedium in that fate. And I beg to be tested on this!

Perhaps I have failed to stray far from the apartment today so that I might avoid encountering other people. By staying out of the busy markets, I have only seen a few locals who, out of curiosity, look out of their windows as I pass.

2 May 1854

Living in Europe has spoiled me for one thing: the ease of transportation. Wilkinson concluded his business in Tangiers and we travelled by camel caravan to Tetouan. I could not help but feel wistful upon arriving here because from some vantage points my beloved homeland can be seen. How different life can be on either side of such a short expanse of water.

The camel caravan was my first time riding a camel. I think my camel was infatuated with me. She kept looking back over her shoulder and although I do not know for certain what a smiling camel looks like, I do believe she was smiling at me. She couldn't have batted her long eyelash harder!

The city we are in now is filled with startlingly white architecture. It is unlike anything I have seen before. The buildings are cold and blinding in the sun, but beautiful.

Wilkinson has found a very nice apartment for us to stay in. He offered Murtaza a fee to travel with us to continue to be a guide and translator on our journey, but Murtaza declined, wishing to stay in Tangiers to spend long overdue time with his family. With my Arabic skills a disappointment, Wilkinson has assured me that he will find us a new guide tomorrow so that we will not be taken advantage of in this city. The reputation here is even more shady that that of Tangiers, despite the brilliant clean look of the city.

3 May 1854

Although I should be getting used to his ways by now, it still amazes me that Wilkinson is able to find young women with such ease. I thought perhaps I would be able to spend my first full day in Tetouan exploring the city, maybe even traveling by camel down to the shore of the Mediterranean to get an even better glimpse of Spain, but Wilkinson put me to work as soon as I had the slightest bit of food in me. Afternoons are my own, mornings and evenings I am not a free man. Wilkinson did keep his word, though, and hired a guide who I was able to meet in the afternoon once I had completed my "patient" examinations.

4 May 1854

Shame! I cannot even look at my own reflection for the overwhelming shame I feel. How long have I been in this man's company and I have already let his ideas infect me thus?

It started off much like our days in Tangiers: A parade of young women, many no older than Rosemary. After about six of these pathetic beings, I was greeted by an intoxicating aroma unlike anything I have ever smelled. The holy slut who entered my room seemed to be bathed in fragrant oil. She bore a striking resemblance to my fair Grace, only of a darker complexion. She had the same smile. The same happy gleam in her eye, oblivious to her fate.

As I performed my examination, I noticed that my hand trembled and a bead of sweat dripped down my face. How could I turn this girl over to Wilkinson? Like his own perfect daughter, he would not appreciate her rare beauty. He would not treat her like she deserved. He would use her today and toss her aside tomorrow. I began to hope that I would find something wrong during my examination, the slightest thing so that I might be able to justify turning her away and moving on to the next. But I found nothing wrong. She was strong. She was vital. She was ready.

I thought about lying to Wilkinson, but I had heard stories of the girls who we turned away in Tangiers being beaten for not being good enough for the rich businessman. If I turned her away for a lie, would I be sending her to an even worse fate? No. I had to present her to Wilkinson.

Wilkinson studied her very carefully, and for the first time since beginning our business arrangement, he turned the girl away. He must have also seen the resemblance to Grace. What relief I felt to know that this fair creature would not be subjected to Wilkinson's humiliation. As I escorted her from the room, Wilkinson made the offer to me, which he had made every day. Normally it was that I could keep screening the cattle until I found one who suited my fancy, but today that if I found this one appealing, I was welcome to have her. Just have her wait while I continued screening the other girls for him.

Never before had this proposition been remotely tempting, but having been away from Grace for so long, having not felt the loving touch of a woman's hand since moving to London, having been exposed to such debauchery in Wilkinson's employ... That aroma. That smile. If I closed my eyes and ran my fingers through her hair could I imagine that it was Grace? It was too much for me to resist.

Demon! This man has corrupted me! That I could stray so easily in my devotion to Grace is only possible because of my prolonged exposure to the wrongdoing I have seen Wilkinson pass off as acceptable, respectable behaviour. As soon as my carnal desires had been satisfied, I sent the girl away, angry at her, angry at myself!

I must resolve to be more diligent in my devotion to Grace. To not give in to temptation again, for I fear that the temptations will only increase the longer I am away from England, the longer I am in these foreign lands, surrounded by new smells, new sites, exotic beauty.

Grace can never find out about this.

Home. My homeland. I can see it from here. Is it still my home? Am I still the same man I was when I left there? I do not even feel like the same man who left England only a few short weeks ago. How much I have seen, yet how little I have seen! How much more there still is to see and experience. It is not uncommon for a man to grow up and only ever live within one mile of his family home for his entire existence. One day's walk is the farthest he will travel, and yet here I am, not only living in a foreign land but traveling to places I had previously never heard of.

Is this good for my soul? Should a man set down roots? Stay home, with his parents nearby so that he can contribute to their care in their dotage? If I had stayed home, I wouldn't be the person I am now, but would that be better? Would the Diego of Andalusia have been so easily tempted? Succumb without a care to his physical desire, despite his better judgment?

I yearn for a home. A place where I can raise my family and make my name. A wife. Love. Some days, like today, I look at what I'm doing and I wonder if any of this is attainable if I stay on my current path.

To cross that narrow passage, get on the next ferry and go home... Would that be giving up? What does life in Spain hold for me? Especially life in Andalusia with my family? Family. I miss my sister dearly, but my parents have always been oppressive. Each day with them is an exercise in endurance. Is that how I want my life to play out? Hoping as I wake up each morning that I can simply survive through to the night? At least away from home I can have bigger goals. I can dream of doing important things. Perhaps even do good! Mary and Thomas need help. Felicity needs help. If I am able to provide them the help they desperately need, then leaving Spain was the right decision, no matter how challenging my life seems right now.

Does Isabel feel content each night to look upon Antonio's sleeping face and know that he will be there with her when she wakes up and that their lives will continue the same ad infinitum? Perhaps becoming a mother will provide Isabel with a more profound sense of fulfilment, and who's to say that as a father Antonio won't experience the same? Just because I cannot fathom that having children would be enough to satisfy my desire to be...VITAL...it doesn't mean that for some people it isn't enough.

And so, despite the deep shame I feel, I cannot get on the next ferry to Spain. I cannot get on any ferry to Spain unless it is a ferry that Wilkinson orders me to get on. My life, my home, is no longer the same as my homeland. It will always hold a place in my heart. It will always be the place that my thoughts turn to in my darkest hours of despair, but it I cannot live there.

5 May 1854

What wonders a good night's sleep can do. Yesterday now seems like a bad dream which over time will be forgotten.

This morning I find myself with a much clearer head, although perhaps "clear" is not the correct term. My mind swirled so last night that the only solace I could find was an overindulgence in alcohol. Unfortunately, this only endeared me further to Wilkinson who I encountered as I left the apartment late last night. He thought the idea of a nightcap sounded delightful and decided to go with me. Perhaps it was my good fortune that he did accompany me, for the city was filled with strange sounds and I would swear I always saw someone moving just out of range of my vision, perhaps following me? Regardless, I did not feel safe roaming the city streets so late, and had I been on my own I would have felt even less so, especially not knowing where to go to find what I sought.

The result is that this morning my head aches unlike ever before in my life! I have no idea what it was that I drank last night. I do not want to know. If I never encounter it again my life will be all the better. I spent what coherent moments I had last night thinking about that girl. The way she smelled. That was the source of her irresistible hold on me. I see it now. The fragrance she wore blinded me to my own true love so that I forgot myself. My inhibitions were released and I was helpless.

I must find this girl again and have a sample of the potion she wore! Out of my shameful behaviour, my love of science is renewed! Whatever other samples I have collected thus far, this scent is the most amazing. I must find her. I must have it.

8 May 1854

I was beginning to fear that fortune had turned her back on me for good. Today is our last day in Tetouan. Tomorrow at dawn we board the steamer once more and head to Egypt. Farther east as our voyage continues. I had begun to lose hope of finding the young woman of my indiscretion after several days of searching. It was surprisingly easy for Wilkinson to navigate the underbelly of society, but it was a role I was not as comfortable in and one where I wasn't taken seriously. People were difficult and uncooperative as I interviewed them, hoping to learn the whereabouts of this girl whose name I did not even know.

Today, at what felt like the last possible moment, I found her. She wore the same perfume, so that before even looking upon her I was able to confirm that I had found my prize as my nose led me through the darkened bar. Perhaps because I was aware of the potential affect her potent aroma could have on me, I was able to stave off its effects and was not so blindly swayed by lust as when I first encountered her and it. Or perhaps it was because at the moment I was a man on a mission – to find out the origin of her secret and make it my own.

She laughed when I asked her so gravely what her perfume was, thinking me capricious for seeking her out for this purpose and not because I wished to bed her again. She had been aware that I was searching for her, but did not want to meet me until she was ready. Although she was surprised at the true reason why I had gone to such lengths to find her, she nonetheless made it worth her time by charging me a fee for the information I was after. The source of her perfume was a tree resin known as olibanum which was steamed to produce an aromatic oil which could then be applied to the skin as a perfume. For an additional fee, she told me that I could find the raw form of olibanum in the market, describing the look of it (small almost white stones, cloudy and irregular in shape) in case I had any difficulty remembering the name or communicating with the vendors.

With haste I made my way back to the market and was able to purchase an ample supply of olibanum for future study. The stones are small and will not be difficult to transport, and perhaps this is for the best that I was not able to buy the perfumed oil as glass jars might break on the long voyage still to come while a purse of stones will suffer little damage. Still, the result is that I cannot begin to fully explore the potential of this substance until I return home and am able to set up a laboratory where I can learn the vital elements which give this substance its power.

Tomorrow our journey continues, for good or bad, but I feel now at least there might be some reason for me to be on these travels. There is hope that I am not only going to encounter empty folktales, but that some of the purported magic might be real. I have felt the power myself, been touched by the wonders of this untamed land, and, today at least, I do have faith that good will come of this.

Upon seeing her again, she did look like Grace...

CHAPTER 3 - EGYPT

12 May 1854

My dearest Isabel,

Such wonders have I seen! I have done my best to capture these marvels on paper so that you might have some taste of the incredible journey I have been on. We arrived in Egypt at the port city of Alexandria and were greeted by the stone-faced Sphinx. Our steamer turned right down the Nile and we sailed inland to Giza and Cairo. We have settled in here for a brief stay before continuing our journey. Our next leg will be our most challenging, as we will actually have to travel over land, abandoning the relative safety of the sea as we cross due east to Suez. From there Lord Wilkinson has arranged for us to be met by a new contingent of ships as we continue our journey by sea.

The banalities of my day to day work are not worth tiring you with. Instead I must say how thankful I am to have you in my life to remind me to take the time to explore this alien landscape and see it through fresh eyes – not the tired eyes of a physician who only gets to have a few hours to himself in the late day once his work is complete. I seek out excitement and beauty so that I may pass it along to you.

In Giza I have also been able to see the Pyramids! We take for granted that our lives are so modern and our technology so advanced, yet seeing these awe-inspiring, imposing structures one cannot help but marvel at just how little we know. These incredible architectural wonders have been standing for thousands of years before I even came into existence. My words are inadequate when confronted with this miracle of man. I wish you could see it. This is my favourite stop so far, and I long to linger here, but I know already that Lord Wilkinson plans for our stay here to be the briefest of any on our voyage.

I know that my sketches cannot begin to convey the true spectacle of the Sphinx and the Pyramids, but I wanted to share my small triumph with you. Although I daren't say that my drawings are showing any marked improvement in my artistic talent level, through my diligent efforts my confidence has grown and a sketch which only a few weeks ago might have taken me an hour I'll now complete in a fraction of the time. My enjoyment at drawing has increased proportionally as my struggle to draw has decreased. To be able to go to the Pyramid and see it and sketch it and have my drawing not only be a reasonable facsimile of what I see, but to be able to capture it so much more quickly— How encouraging this is!

As I was roaming through the city the other day, I thought about how different my experience would be if you were at my side. I do enjoy exploring and meeting new people. Experiencing the culture. Tasting the foods, smelling the odours... But there is an overwhelming part of me which longs to share these times with someone. When I finish my work for Lord Wilkinson, we part ways until evening when we reconnect for a late supper. This time of the afternoon and early evening is all my own and I find that it has become increasingly lonely.

I am not even remotely suggesting that you should feel sorry for me! Here I am, traveling the world, seeing things which most people can only dream of, and yet the experience is teaching me above all else the value of having someone with whom to share the quiet moments of life. And there you are. How long now until you are a mother? Until your life takes on a deeper meaning which I may never be able to understand? Do you envy me the freedom of being able to roam? I envy you for your strength and stability.

When I look back on these travels, who will I share my memories with? I certainly do not delude myself into thinking that I will one day in my dotage sit by a fire with Lord Wilkinson and reminisce about our wonderful travels together. He is but a temporary visitor in my life and unless he becomes family through the bond of marriage, I am uncertain as to how long our acquaintance will last.

Our journey will soon continue and I will ride a camel across the desert to a distant sea. A camel! And, surprising as it may seem to you, this will not be my first time to do so. I am becoming an exceptionally skilled camel rider!

I will write again. Although I will not get your reply for what seems like an eternity, knowing you are there is a source of endless comfort for me.

All my love,

Diego

12 May 1854

Wanderlust has long been my master. I could have taken a wife in Spain and if I had, how different it would all be. But why burden myself with these questions now. Here I am, in yet another foreign land and it is teaching me one thing above all else – I am lonely. As I leave my room each morning, I imagine that Grace calls out to me, reminding me to take care of myself on my travels. Telling me that I should put on a hat if I'm going to be in the sun, or that perhaps it will be too warm to wear a scarf. My own conscious has taken her voice so that as I wait for sleep to claim me each night. I have conversation with her. How disappointed I shall be when I have one of these conversations in truth and the details I have ascribed to her life do not match up with how her life really is. Or, perhaps the details of her life are more wondrous than I can even imagine.

Not all of my thoughts are pure. There are moments when I find myself thinking about her and realize that I have allowed my mind to wander. Such an innocent, delicate creature should not be subjected to such thoughts, yet I cannot stop myself from imagining...

She is so beautiful. So refined. The curve of her neck. The bowing of her lips...

13 May 1854

Vital! That is how I feel today.

I must remind myself continually that looking at the human body, particularly the female body, is something to be cherished. By my profession I am permitted access to secret realms otherwise reserved for a spouse or God. I have seen naked flesh from angles most men do not have the imagination to consider, and yet so many days this is nothing more than my job. I look at these women as a shepherd looks at his sheep, or a scholar at his books. This is my trade; these are the tools.

When I think of Grace I am reminded of just how beautiful and miraculous the human body can be, and it shakes me from the haze and I look upon my patients with clearer thoughts and fully open, appreciative eyes. But this trip with Wilkinson has been trying and I struggle to retain this perspective.

Today I did not examine a stream of women. Since arriving in Cairo our entire routine has changed. Wilkinson spends most of the day making arrangements for the continuation of our journey across Asia so that he doesn't have time to bring me women to examine. He is tired in the afternoons and retires to his room to nap until it is time to dine, at which time I must go collect him so that we can dine together. Whatever business he was carrying out in Tangiers and Tetouan does not continue here in Cairo and so as one detail has changed, all details have changed.

This leaves my days carefree. It is unfortunate that we will not linger here, but it is best that I not dwell on this fact. Instead I must cling to the hope that other stops on our journey might be as this one, where I am free to do as I please. And where there are remarkable things to see.

I went to the marketplace today and found it to be similar to those in Morocco. Vendors selling mysterious items of unknown origin, purported to cure ills which had no cure or needed no cure. Magic. I found several vendors selling olibanum and was surprised to hear the folktales surrounding this stone-like resin. From my own experience I am sure it is a powerful aphrodisiac, but the salesmen assured me its purpose is to cleanse the spirit, removing physical and emotional impurities.

The harvesting of olibanum has much to do with the legend. A tree is cut and where it is cut, it weeps. These tears turn to stone, which is the olibanum. The stories say that as the stones were formed from the tree's tears, taking its pain and healing its bark, so the olibanum takes the pain away from those who wear the oil on their skin.

I'll continue to seek folktales on this topic, as I am not convinced this is the only use. There must be more stories, stories which the vendors I encountered hadn't heard.

The market also had the cobra charmers with their baskets. It was thanks to one of these charmers, a young man who still hasn't learned all of the tricks of his trade, that I was able to feel useful today.

He couldn't have been more than eighteen years old, but already well versed in the theatrics of duping tourists out of the money. This snake charmer, to his own detriment, had spent more time perfecting his rapport with the crowd than with the snakes, and as a result he had a rather nasty bite on his arm from a recent run in with one of his pets.

Feeling some obligation to keep the secrets of charmers everywhere, I did not interrupt his show, but I could see that he had not sought proper treatment for the bite and the pain on his face was obvious. Nursing a painful (potentially fatal) wound might be good for business, convincing the crowd of the danger involved in his job, but without better care it would be a victory short-lived.

Once the crowd had dispersed, I insisted on examining his wound. Necrosis had already begun on the skin around the bite, but debridement was possible. Treating the charmer in the marketplace was far from sanitary, but it provided the best possible conditions in other ways. Whatever items I needed to treat him, if they were not in my bag, I could easily procure them. And it provided excellent entertainment while we waited for the binding cloth to dry. Once it was dry, the dead skin came away easily and it was with great relief that we saw the skin underneath was not infected to such a degree that all hope was lost for being able to save his arm.

I was able to clean the wound properly, and since he hadn't succumbed to the neurotoxins when the bite was originally inflicted, the danger of the venom had passed. It will be his own responsibility to care for the wound until it is fully healed, but I was able to show him how and I am confident he will heal well enough in time. And, if he suffers a similar fate in his future dealings with cobras, more bites and exposure to the venom, he will now be able to treat his own wounds with a great deal more success.

There are days when I question my whole existence. And then there are days like today. No thought of compensation. No thought of right or wrong. Just doing what I was put on Earth to do. Helping my fellow man heal.

How pretentious I must sound! But how glorious it is to know that this young man's life, his livelihood, will continue because I was able to help.

These days are too few and I must cherish them when they come along.

15 May 1854

Camels! I think I am going to dream about camels for days to come. Will I never get this smell out of my nose?

I look back over the words I wrote the day before last, and I remind myself that each day is to be cherished, no matter how trying or absurd it seems at the time. How many of my days will be spent riding a camel through the desert? (Two more, providing things go well, and I imagine the same on my return journey.) But out of a whole lifetime of days, the number is insignificant. Each bump, each blister should be remembered. Noted as a once in a lifetime experience, because it is just that. I will pass sand and rocks and lizards tomorrow under a blazing sun, but it will not be the same sand and rocks and lizards I passed today. Millions of grains of sand, all unique. Each to be appreciated.

Our guides, whether they remember our particular journey with them or not, had a good laugh at my expense today. While in Tangiers I did find a good supply of peppermint candies which I had been using as a folk remedy to stave off my seasickness. I expected to have enough for the next sea leg of our journey, but found an unexpected need for them today. I do not know why my first camel trip did not cause me to become ill from the motion (a back and forth swaying which is similar to the swishing of ocean waves), but today it proved to be too much for me to overcome. The camels were quite content to travel a great distance without stopping, but I had to insist that our caravan stop several times so that I could be sick, not wanting to vomit off the back of the camel. Without the peppermints I fear it would have been even worse, although the thought is hard to imagine. I will have to procure more mints, or some other remedy for motion sickness in Suez.

Tonight, we have made camp in the desert. This is the first time since beginning our journey where we truly are experiencing life removed from the comforts of Europe. The apartments we stayed in prior to this, the places where we would dine in the evenings, they were all influenced by European culture. Designed to make traders, businessmen and expatriates, comfortable in this strange land. Out here there are no comforts. The only thing between me and the heartless desert is a canvas tent.

I have had to seclude myself temporarily to recover from my day. There is no doctor to come in and look after me, so I must be cautious and not let my own health suffer. I must remain resilient.

Already the aroma of cooking food has begun to waft through the air. It is restorative. I am confident that tonight will be one of the best meals I have ever had in my life. True food. Food prepared by hungry, tired men to satisfy a hunger that does not come from easy city life, but that can only be experienced out here in the desert. The scent of it alone is intoxicating. I feel like I haven't eaten in days (although the quantity of food expelled from my stomach throughout the day proves otherwise)!

Hallelujah. The smell of camels may not be driven from my nose, but the roasting meat will allay it for the time being.

16 May 1854

I have made friends with my camel. We've come to an understanding where I will do a better job of riding her, and she will not make me quite as sick from the movement. We are both happier for it, me for not having to suck on mints all day, her for not having me yank on the reins until the bolt is almost coming out of her nose. Not a pleasant situation for either of us. I also didn't need the caravan to make the frequent stops like I did yesterday.

As we camp this evening it is Wilkinson who is letting the desert get the better of him. I have spent enough of our days in Africa out in the sun, allowing it to darken my skin so that with proper attire (and a firmly closed lip) I might even pass as a native. If my life depended on it, it is a charade which would have some chance of success. Wilkinson has spent most of his time indoors, and so has not had the same benefit of gradual sun exposure, instead getting heavy doses all at once these past two days. He has turned such a vivid shade of red that if he were to cut his face no one would see the blood, it would simply appear the same colour as his skin.

It is much to Wilkinson's good fortune to be traveling with this caravan. Once camp was made, I was able to obtain some camel's milk and made a cool compress for his face to help relieve the pain. He will need to remain inside his tent with the compress applied the rest of the night so that he is able to resume our journey tomorrow. To help calm his mind, I was also able to find an ample supply of wine. My secret weapon! How many ills have I treated by simply having my patient drown their sorrows in alcohol until the sorrows were forgotten?

Wilkinson insisted that I join him in the libations, and I surprised myself at how easily I was persuaded. Neither one of us had eaten dinner yet (I could hear the men outside still preparing our evening meal), and soon we were both quite intoxicated. I kept enough of my wits about me to remind Wilkinson to keep the compress on his face. The alcohol loosened Wilkinson's tongue considerably.

I left him unattended briefly once the call rang out that dinner was ready, returning only a few moments later with a plate for each of us. During that time, he managed to remove the compress and had I returned an instant later I would have found him in a heap on the floor rather than resting in his cot. I quickly rushed to his aid, and while arranging him (he was gangly and uncooperative), I discovered, to my dismay, that he was quite well armed.

My hand slipped around to his back to help pull him safely onto the cot and there in the small of his back was a revolver – well-concealed from me for our entire journey thus far. I would hope that if our travels were through dangerous lands where such a weapon was necessary for protection that Wilkinson would have either provided me with my own weapon or at least had the decency to warn me that it might be wise to obtain one. The fact that he did no such thing made me question even more what kind of business he's in. Something so dangerous where he feels it is necessary to keep a weapon so close, even as he settles on his cot for the night.

What did he talk about... Already my mind is foggy as sleep begins to settle upon me, but I will try my best to document his ramblings. He revealed to me that although Robert had been away in France, he was serving in the military and that as soon as it began to look inevitable that he would be sent off to the war taking place on the Crimean Peninsula, Wilkinson stepped in and exerted his formidable political power, getting Robert released from all military obligations. In general, I'm opposed to the idea of shirking one's duty to country, but having met Robert the decision was a wise one for both Robert and England alike.

The war was having a considerable effect on Wilkinson's life. He revealed to me that part of his business normally would be to travel to Russia in the spring, searching for amber. The lightweight, yet valuable stones were amongst his favourites. Travel across Europe was not as difficult as our current journey thanks to recent advances in railways, and he was well-established in his trade, making his trips exceedingly profitable. I surmise that our current journey also involves gems in some capacity (which explains why I have yet to see him with any substantial cargo).

 Lady Wilkinson was spoken of fondly. I find it fascinating that Wilkinson is able to express such love for her and still carry on the way he does while away from home. While only a short distance from home!

He hopes that David will marry Grace. The families have been making arrangements for their union their entire lives, hoping that once they were both of age that nothing would bar their joining together. He anticipates that this summer all of the elements will come together and by fall he'll be planning a wedding. This news makes my frustration over being away on this extended journey even greater!

Just as Wilkinson was recounting one of his escapades with a Russian whore, he dozed off. I checked his compress, made sure he was secure in his cot and took my leave.

How can I fight against an unseen enemy? My words, no matter how loudly I shout them, no matter how sincere, cannot be heard over such a great distance. I could make a bold move and write to her, but she does not know me, and doing so would probably scare her away before she even gives me a chance.

Why should she believe that I love her? What proof can I offer of what is in my heart? To have known someone for such a short time, to only have experienced them through fleeting glances and impersonal conversation, surely she does not yet share my feelings and if I push too hard, I risk losing her forever. Capturing her heart is like capturing a butterfly. I must be quiet. Still. Patient. Wait for the butterfly to land on my finger, not go chasing it all over the yard – running the risk of tiring myself out and injuring it in the pursuit.

18 May 1854

My Dearest Isabel,

As I write this to you, I am once again at sea. After a three-day ride through the desert, I was sad to say goodbye to my camel. We had grown quite fond of each other and I swear she shed a tear as we parted ways! When my nephew is old enough, we'll have to plan a trip together across the Mediterranean so that he can ride a camel.

I need so desperately to talk to you. Although I am surrounded by people, and not so much the outsider as I was in London, I have never felt as alone as I have the past few days. My camel was good company, but she could not drive this shadow from my spirit.

I suppose it is an inevitable side effect of love. Before meeting Grace, I was blissfully unaware of what it was like to desire something so strongly. I needed to eat, so I ate. I felt like stretching my legs, so I would go for a walk. I occasionally found myself lacking for conversation, but a strategically chosen table in the pub or park bench, and I could listen to other people discuss the concerns of their daily lives. But now I am in a situation where I need to talk to someone, and no matter who I talk to the feeling does not abate. It is increasingly clear that it is not "someone" I need to talk to, it is Grace and no other person on Earth, in London, in Spain, in Africa, at sea, and soon in India, will do.

The ache in my soul (as a physician, I cannot discern the location more accurately than this) is unbearable at times. My mood swings, though. Tonight, I will stand on deck and watch as the sun sets behind our ship and I know that the beauty of the water and the sun and the sense of isolation will be overwhelming. Perhaps I will weep at the splendour of the scene. All the while I will long for Grace to be at my side, to share the moment with me.

I do not wish to be morbid, but it gives me comfort to share these feelings with you.

Living alone, life is so simple. I am my own man. I do what I want, can be capricious, and it only affects me. If I decide to walk away from Lord Wilkinson at the next port, fend for myself in Bombay, I have the ability to do so. I answer to no one. There is great freedom, and great fear in that. I am free to go where I want, to do what I want. I surround myself with "friends," but eventually we tire of each other and part ways. There is no shame or hurt feeling in this. It is just how life is. The friendships are not to be sustained. They serve their purpose in the moment, and then when the conversation becomes strained, they end.

But what on this Earth, then, keeps me from walking off of this ship as we sail across the sea? Keeps me from roaming into the desert, away from the caravan, without enough water to last the night? You? Grace? Our parents?

The idea that our parents keep me sane is horrifying! How tragic if my entire life hangs in the balance, depending on my most tenuous relationship. And Grace, although I love her dearly, thus far only occupies my hopes and dreams. I must assume that you are the force in my life which I hold dear above all others. You are what keeps me here, keeps me from doing something rash. Keeps me working and striving, and keeps Andalusia in my heart as home. But I long for something which you cannot offer. I do not mean to offend you, but you must understand that a sister's love is not what I'm speaking of, although it keeps me bound safely to reason.

Out of this whole world, we all search for the one other person who we will not tire of. Where, if the conversation becomes strained, we can sit together in silence until the tension has passed and we can once again speak freely, unencumbered by societal rules of propriety. We are just "we." Not always of one mind, not always of one spirit, but always of one desire – to sustain our connection. During the difficult patches, we know that they will not last forever, but they give us strength, making our bond even stronger.

Is this an idealized view? You, dear sister, are living this miracle. Tell me! Is Antonio your other half? Do you fight, knowing that once the fight is over your relationship will be all the stronger, like metal being tempered by coming through the fire? How comforting it must be. To have someone to stand beside you. To know that if things get rough, you will not have to weather the storm alone. To have someone who depends on you, making you work harder each day to do more, to be better, must be invigorating.

Now I must go watch that sunset. I'll think of you and Antonio doing the same.

ELIXIR

All my love,

Diego

CHAPTER 4 - JAPAN

(not dated)

I've come to plead my case before the goddess

Born from water, born from wind, born from foam

Though my heart has always yearned to wander

Through my roaming, my heart has found its home

In the darkness, every night, the gentle rocking

of the waves condemns my soul to restless sleep

A secret prisoner, no other chains are needed

Bound by the insurmountable expanse of the deep

Within this finite exile is there a Rubicon,

past which, dear Venus, you offer me no aid?

Time away from love's fair breath, I ache

But does love use time against me and so fade?

What prize can win my maiden's hand?

Golden apples growing from the tree?

Precious gems? Silken ribbons? Ambergris?

It matters not while my heart is trapped at sea

What more must I do to prove my worth?

Venus, don't you find my love sincere?

Am I not worthy of your interest? Your time?

I'll ask you just this once to interfere

The sound of her voice does not abate

The image of her face I can't erase

The burning deep inside intensifies

Take pity on me please, for love of Grace

23 June 1854

I had to ask in a shop what day it was today. Since we first made land in India, I have been the slave of my new mistress: alcohol. My days are short, performing my work quickly with my head pounding, my shoulders and heart heavy, until I am able to meet my concubine for our secret daily rendezvous. How secret it has been, I do not know and I do not care.

How many days of my life have I squandered? Lost in a haze, never to be returned? And yet as I consider this, I wonder if there really would have been value in living those days. Here, so far away from home now, what joy I once found in my travels has evaporated. My only goal now is to get through, to make it to the next day so that I can once again carry on my tumultuous affair.

India, gone. Malacca, Sumatra, Java, Borneo, the Philippines, all gone. What makes today different from so many days which have gone before?

I don't remember much of the past month. I have somehow managed to continue to collect various folk medicine objects. My trunks are brimming with potions and samples. Items to be tested, some with instructions scrawled on bits of paper, carefully wrapped about them so as not to be misplaced.

I am in Japan, this much I know. I have kept a vague awareness at all times about my general geographic location. Perhaps I am alert today because I know that our journey is nearing an end. Once Wilkinson completes his business here, we return to sea and head back to England. Our stops will be for supplies only. No more extended stays. With all haste we will head...home.

So why is today different? My head is...clear. My memories of last night's nocturnal activities are just as hazy as if seen through my comfortable drunken stupor, yet for all the intoxicated feeling, I do not recall ever stopping for a drink. I must piece together what fragments I can to solve this mystery.

Wilkinson came to collect me at half past ten. We wound our way through the streets to this small underground establishment where, to my surprise, the Madam of the house was just that, a madame. French. I had given little thought to how Wilkinson would manage to find his amusement in this land. His ingenuity has long since ceased to amaze me in this regard. Although we only arrived and Wilkinson's guide and translator had yet to present himself, I had no doubt that Wilkinson would already have long-established contacts making his hobby just as easy to carry out here as it had been in all of the other just-as-mysterious places we had already visited.

Now that I think about it, perhaps I should have found it odd that for this stop we were going to a brothel. This was not part of Wilkinson's normal procedure, preferring to have the girls discreetly come to him. But I had only one thought in my head that morning. The same thought which had consumed me for so many weeks – to get through my first few hours of the day on the very edge of sobriety so that once Wilkinson was satisfied, I could leap off that cliff and drown in the bitter deep waters of inebriation. Another day done in a blink and one day closer to home.

Perhaps it was the atmosphere of the place... After spending such a long time surrounded by things which are so foreign, to be here in this haven of European delights was so welcomed. I found comfort there as soon as I entered. After all I have done to resist Wilkinson's influence, the most at ease I have felt on this journey is when I stepped foot into a den of ill repute. Has my soul been corrupted so thoroughly that this is truly where I belong?

Madam DuPont instantly recognized Wilkinson. She whisked us to a small back room where she consulted a ledger which listed all of her clients' visits since her business began. With amazing accuracy, she flipped through the pages and found Wilkinson's entry. "It has been quite a while," she said as she ran a long bony finger down the page. She looked up at Wilkinson with a hungry grin. "Same girl as last time?"

Wilkinson balked at the idea, as did I. Madam DuPont immediately sensed that Wilkinson had little interest in the same old bit of stuff he'd had who knows (well, I don't know, but Madam DuPont did) how many years earlier. "Ah. Her younger sister, perhaps? She's the very image." At this idea Wilkinson closed his eyes and sank momentarily into his memory of the young girl he had met in a past visit. When he returned to us the smile on his face was all the answer Madam DuPont needed.

I began to speak, to remind Wilkinson that he brought me along not just for companionship, but before I even finished uttering a sentence, he silenced me and assured me that my services were not needed in my professional capacity. He had brought me along because out of all of his experiences, his travels, this brothel was the best in the world and that no man could forgive himself for not taking advantage of stopping in for a visit.

From here my mind can only remember vaguely what happened. Wilkinson was taken away by a woman who wore a white garment as thin as spiderweb. It clung to her perfect body, showing every ripple of her muscles beneath her skin as they flexed and contracted with her movements. The smile never left her face. I began to feel giddy, returning my attention to Madam DuPont. Had I misjudged this woman when I first saw her? The longer I looked at her the more alluring she became. Mysterious. Provocative. My inhibitions began to slip away and the thought of staying in this lion's den and allowing this woman to choose a concubine for me no longer seemed as distasteful as it should. It actually started to seem like a good idea.

This woman, with her long bony fingers, and her long thin face, her tall narrow frame, did we pass the hours together? As I recall her now, I see a different picture than I did yesterday. Her skin so pale as to almost be white. Her eyes deep set giving her the hollowest, almost dead expression. Her hair equally as thin as the rest of her, piled high atop her head. There is another face in my mind's eye. Smiling. Lovely. But I only catch fleeting glimpses of her.

I don't remember accepting a drink, but I have no doubt that I was slipped some kind of poison. No, not a poison. An elixir. I felt at ease in this strange place, the most relaxed I have since beginning this journey. Whatever transpired I am certain of one thing – it was the most pleasurable experience of my life.

That I could remember it more clearly! Is Madam DuPont a sorceress who has put me under a spell?

This morning I find the scientist within reawakened, longing to know what caused such ecstasy. Was there incense burning? Is that how I was so drugged? Was it Madam DuPont's perfume? Upon initial whiff it seemed so stale and dense, but perhaps it has this power. Or was it Madam DuPont herself? Is she so skilled at her trade that she can mesmerize a man so thoroughly?

I wouldn't be surprised if the entire purpose of the trip was this place. Wilkinson's "business" was merely a front for this elaborate world tour which ultimately lead to the small French brothel in Japan where a weary traveller could experience bliss unlike any other on earth.

I am vexed by my own mind. I possess the awareness that yesterday was filled with unimaginable pleasure, but the details are nowhere to be found. Perhaps I imagined the whole thing. What a nice trick Madam DuPont has for herself – drug the men who knock on her door, show them to a bed and leave them alone to dream up their own bliss.

Wilkinson has not come to rouse me yet this morning. Are we going back there today? Already I anticipate a return. Two days ago, had I been told of my current frame of mind I would have screamed liar! And yet, here I am. Here I am.

24 June 1854

What horrible dreams I had last night! I have had the odd bad dream in my day, but the dreams I experienced last night were so vivid. So real.

I was back in London, in my flat. Just roused from sleep by an unfamiliar noise. I felt something move across the foot of my bed. A pressure, not unlike a hand pressing on the mattress, pushing against it to stand. Then I was seized by that terror which overcomes me when I first awaken from a nightmare. The fear to move, the fear to breathe.

I wonder what causes this fear? A dream long forgotten, and yet there is this uncertainty which overcomes me which makes me afraid to open my eyes and look out into the room. A fear that a cat burglar has made his way in and stands above me with a steel pipe, ready to attack the moment my eyes flick open. My only hope of survival is to keep my eyes closed and remain perfectly still.

In my dream I had this feeling. And as happens when I'm awake, I began to discuss the situation with myself. I was alone. I heard no noise. Each moment I spent awake not moving was further proof that everything was okay. A cat burglar would be making noise. Breathing. He would get bored standing over a sleeping man and would take a step. The passing moments of continued silence where all I could hear was my own blood pulsing through my veins was assurance it was safe to at least open my eyes. I didn't need to move; just open my eyes and I would see that everything was okay.

I opened my eyes and as I stared at the ceiling, willing myself to turn my head to look at some more useful part of the room, I felt the pressure on the bed again, this time closer to my knees, moving in a sweeping motion. I was not alone. Was I being toyed with? I steeled myself and tilted my head to look toward the foot of the bed, to stare the intruder in the face, but as I moved, a sharp pain ran through my body.

I could feel the fangs of the giant beast as they dug deeply into my thigh. The cobra of my nightmare bore little resemblance to those I had encountered in India. It was as wide around as my own torso. Its massive caped head was up on my bed, making a meal of my lower half, but its tail had barely cleared the door. I struggled to break free from those massive fangs, but no matter which way I turned, the creature held tight.

I scanned the room looking for a weapon to fight off this mindless attacker, yet none could be found. I reached down and began to wrestle the snake with my bare hands. I could feel the venom rushing through my body. I managed to pry the beast off and pulled its head up to mine, forgetting a most vital piece of information I had learned about cobras. As I stared my tormentor in the eyes, it spit. The venom hit my eyes, blinding me and causing a second rush of pain through my body. Had I been awake, I have no doubt at this point I would have passed out – if not long before now.

Instead, I awoke. I was sweating profusely. And I was afraid to move. Afraid to open my eyes.

As usual, time was my best ally in the fight against this irrational fear. I stayed perfectly still, knowing that I would either tire myself out and fall back asleep (the sun had yet to rise) or I would satisfy myself knowing that there were no noises in the room, that I was in Japan, not London, and that I was, as always, perfectly alone.

I fell back asleep, but when I finally awoke the memory of the dream was just as vivid as it had been when I awoke the first time. The sun greeted me and the fear had worn off, but the image of that horrific cobra lingers.

I did manage a trip back to Madam DuPont's after being released from my duties for the day and was somewhat put off by the reception I received. No sooner had I entered the establishment than I was asked to leave. "Nothing personal, dearie," she cooed, her accent thick like treacle. Nothing personal? Being turned away by a whore? I protested and she gave me some excuse about coming back in a week, that I wasn't ready for another visit. As if I didn't know my own mind! She placed a clammy hand on my wrist and lead me to the door with surprising strength. I had no interest in causing a scene (my interest was more obvious given my location), so I complied with Madam's wishes.

I wonder now if I could have forced the situation. Perhaps my memory of events has skewed them in my mind, but now that I think back on that grip it was curiously forceful.

I waited outside most of the day like a hungry dog by a kitchen door, hoping to catch one of the girls as she was leaving for a small break, a walk perhaps, so I could take the opportunity to exert my influence upon her. Prey upon her more gentle nature and get my visit one way or the other. But no girls left the building all day. Several men paid visits, going in, but I did not see any of them leave. Perhaps there was a second door to the establishment where the men could leave more discreetly.

My damn enthusiasm got the better of me today, I fear. I stayed as long as I could before fatigue and hunger overcame me. Tomorrow, if I'm still overwhelmed by this desire, I'll return later in the evening. Although Wilkinson has scheduled his life to do his recreating during the day, it occurs to me that an establishment such as Madam DuPont's might do better business under the cover of darkness, when a man cannot be seen coming or going, no matter which door he decides to use.

26 June 1854

Did I take notice of the windows when I was inside? I only vaguely recall there being long draperies in the parlour when we first entered. Red? Orange? Black? We paid our visit during the day and yet I do not recall any natural light. The entrance was subterranean, down a flight of stairs, on the shady side of the building. If there were windows, what would they have revealed? Earth? As soon as we entered the solid wooden door was closed behind us, sealing out the outside world – as if nothing else existed.

I returned late last night to try and stage a chance encounter with one of the women as she stepped out for the night, but none left. Not surprisingly, they must all be housed there. But that they never step outside? I again saw several men enter and did not see them leave. I grew bored staring at the front door and decided to take advantage of the shadow of night to give the building a full inspection. My exposure was limited, but based on the outside of the building, it was likely that the place took up the entire basement. The first floor had a main entrance around the corner. I could only see the front hall as I peered through the main entrance, and it did appear that the floor was divided into several flats – business or residential I could not tell. A large stairwell was at the far end of the hall.

There were several tiny windows near to the ground on the perimeter of the building. I circled several times, determining which one was the least conspicuous, got on my hands and knees, and peered inside. Blackness. It was only because of sloppy workmanship that I realized the windows were intentionally blacked out. A splotch of black paint could be seen on the pale sill. Using my fingernail, for I had no other tools handy, I scratched off a small bit of the black paint, but to no avail. The curtains inside were surely blocking my view.

Wilkinson assures me that we will remain in Japan for several weeks, so we will both call on Madam DuPont again, but I fear I will fall under the same spell as before and not be able to remember anything that transpires.

More windows, more blackness. Each window was the same – covered in black paint and most likely curtained from the inside. I felt like a rat, scurrying along the ground, looking for a way to enter a building, unwelcome, to take something which didn't really belong to me.

27 June 1854

Locked doors surround us all every day. Closed windows. Secret papers signed in private offices. Yet there is little desire to unlock those doors or open those windows or read those papers. It is not until the instruction is given that, above all else, you are forbidden to go somewhere, or do something, or see someone, that human nature shows its darker side and what before one was oblivious to is suddenly elevated to the level of obsession.

If you treat a person like a criminal, how long does it take until they begin to behave like a criminal? The soul begins to wrestle with two conflicting forces – the knowledge that it is better to do what you have been told and not cause trouble, and the desire to do what you have been told not to because there must be some reason it has been forbidden. You would not be forbidden from eating an unsavoury meal. There are plenty of unsavoury meals to be had. More than one person could stand in a lifetime. But you could be denied the chance to partake in a rare delicacy. Perhaps it has been reserved for a visiting diplomat, or the cost is beyond what you could afford in ten lifetimes. As soon as it becomes unattainable, it is desired.

It is not the desire which is so dangerous, though. It is the other facility of the human mind – the ability to imagine. Daydreams become scenarios on not only obtaining the object of desire, but they become detailed plans on how it might actually be attained. What is it that stops a person from taking the step and moving their scheme from fantasy into practice? A locked door? With enough practice, I could learn to pick it. A closed window? Nothing a carelessly tossed rock can't overcome.

A blacked-out window? A closed curtain? I encircled the building over and over tonight, scraping off paint, hoping for a glimpse inside. The recent new moon helped assure my anonymity in the night, but I made no real progress. I dirtied my hands, soiled my pants, hurt my knees.

If I exert force, she will not give up her secrets. They must be taken from her without her even knowing it is happening. I must ponder this now, how can I become a thief of secrets?

28 June 1854

I doubt that anyone on earth is as skilled at squandering time as I am. I have only two days remaining before I am able to return to Madam DuPont's and yet my plan on how to proceed has not progressed. I returned last evening and covered my tracks from the previous nights. Black paint restored on all the windows where I had scratched it off. The last thing I need is to successfully open a curtain only to have light stream in revealing that their sanctuary has already been disrupted.

I did, for the first time of my many visits, encounter a man as he was leaving the establishment – for all the good it did me. I asked him what he could remember but he was still under the influence of the house's magic and he just smiled as I interrogated him. Did he remember which girl he saw? Smile. Did they give him anything to drink? Smile. Was there a smoke in the room which may have intoxicated him? Smile. Was this his first visit or one of many? Smile. Smile. Smile. He did not walk with any intent, merely roaming away in a daze.

I have yet to see one of the girls leave.

29 June 1854

Sleep! Oh, that I could sleep. All new ideas, by virtue of being new, present themselves and interesting and valid. Yet once time has set upon them their merits may prove to be less spectacular than originally believed.

Today I endeavoured to find an antidote to a drug which I am not even certain exists. How can I keep my mind clear when I am placed under Madam DuPont's spell? Determined that there must be some potion which could counteract the effects of the mysterious drug, I visited every apothecary in this city, searching for stimulating substances which would prevent me from spending another day in blissful ignorance.

How strange that I would intentionally wish to counter the effects when the experience has become my obsession! Since the visit, I have thought of little else than how I can recapture that feeling. Each day that I have been told I must wait has been a prison term. Now that my sentence is nearing an end, I can think of nothing other than resisting temptation and discovering the secret of it. If I am not successful and my ploy is discovered, I will be banned forever. This I know. But to know what the cause of such elation is, I am willing to take this risk.

I cannot be certain that the cocktail of stimulants I have concocted will counter the effects of Madam DuPont's drug, however it did manage to keep my head reasonably clear while I tried various other known substances today. If it is capable of keeping me from entering into a euphoric stupor from eating opium, it is the best weapon with which I can equip myself.

If I survive another day, that is. The quantity of toxins in my body today is beyond what should be asked of a normal mortal. Yet these are the lengths I have driven myself to in the frenzy to obtain the secret which has been forbidden. Sleep? Perhaps I shall sleep again someday. For now, I must amuse myself as fatigue fights against the pollutants I have ingested, wrestling for control over my psyche. Nature fights to let nature resume its natural course and the drugs carry out a blind instruction to keep me lucid no matter the cost.

The temptation to return and linger outside the place is strong. My fear is that sleep will decide to claim me at an inopportune time. I am better off waiting out the effects here in my room. Isolated. Private.

One more day to survive before my chance. One more day to endure. And now I am tortured by having to also endure this eternal night.

1 July 1854

Partial success. After spending yesterday with a headache to rival that of the morning after my hardest night of drinking and very little memory of anything else which transpired due to sleep deprivation the night before, I once again chanced the mixture of chemicals and was so energized by the time we arrived at Madam DuPont's that I believe the only thing which could have dulled my senses would have been a swift, deadly blow to the head.

Madam DuPont was more amenable to our visit than she had been at our last encounter. She quickly separated Wilkinson and I and showed me to a private room. I began to panic, wondering how long it would take before Madam DuPont noticed that I wasn't succumbing to her drug as expected. Should I mimic the effects? Only...I couldn't recall what the effects were. I couldn't recall much of anything other than the way I felt during the visit. My actions, my behaviours, all forgotten. Those things which would reveal my deception could not be faked.

My only hope was to try to remain calm and give the appearance of being naturally immune to the effects. Calm! That was my only hope. The mixture of stimulating drugs which I had taken was making me jumpy and twitchy. Not only did I need to be keenly aware of what was going on, but also control myself so that I appeared normal!

I was left alone in the room for only a moment before a very pretty young woman entered. She didn't have the same tired look I was so used to in Wilkinson's women. She had a hungry, eager look in her eyes. Like the experience we were about to share wasn't solely for my own pleasure, but that she too would enjoy it immensely.

Smiles. Not just smiles but big, toothy grins. The women in this place smile so much. Are they truly happy? I couldn't help but wonder if it wasn't an unintentional side effect of the drug. However, it was administered, perhaps the girls were equally as influenced as the customers. Yet why would the men be restricted on their ingestion of it while these women are permitted to partake of it freely and continually? They must have developed some level of immunity to it.

I scanned each room looking for possible delivery methods. Stray tendrils of smoke. Incense. Candles. Was I given anything to drink or eat? No. None of these things. Just those infernal smiles. On the previous visit I am certain I thought the smiles were disarming. Charming. This time they were irritating me. Although not lacking in sincerity, they were not smiles of warmth and friendship. More like the smile a cat gives to a mouse just before devouring it. Hungry, greedy smiles.

My girl introduced herself as Juliette. Another French girl. Perhaps inappropriately, I remarked on this, asking if she had moved to Japan on her own or if Madam DuPont had brought her here. I could have sworn I saw a look of confusion briefly overtake Juliette's face as she answered. All of the girls in the house were from France, hand-selected by Madam DuPont. She answered, reluctantly.

I sat down on the bed and waited. Juliette smiled at me again, but she did not approach. I cannot say if the pace at which time seemed to pass -- which rivalled a drop of honey falling from a dripper -- was nothing more than my perception at having taken so many stimulating agents. It seemed an eternity that we just stared at one another. I spoke again, wanting to end the silence which sat in the room. "I place myself in your capable hands," I said. "Do with me what you will."

Much like a dog watching you while you eat, hoping that you will drop a morsel of food its way, Juliette cocked her head to the side as she regarded me. "I don't really remember much of my last visit," I continued. "Did I see you or was it someone else? Is that inappropriate to ask? I don't really do this much. I mean, I am around it a lot. Do you know Wilkinson? He's on your books, so you must know something of him..." And on I went. I did not stop talking for at least five minutes. And she just let me talk.

Finally, Juliette stopped me and excused herself from the room. I didn't question my good fortune in this instead took the opportunity to quickly spring to my feet and rumple the curtains just enough so that a small sliver of the window was exposed. I made certain that you would not notice this unless you were specifically looking for it. Then as quickly as I had leapt up, I returned to my exact position on the bed, waiting for Juliette to return.

When Juliette returned, she was not alone. She brought two more girls with her and they closed in around me. Smiling. Juliette pushed me onto my back and knelt over me. "How are you feeling?" she asked.

Again, I was not able to fully control my tongue and I answered truthfully. Perhaps I have unwittingly not only stumbled upon a powerful stimulant, but one which induces veracity? "I am somewhat tired having not slept well the past few nights. I also feel rather nervous. I wasn't exactly expecting so much attention." I would have willingly continued to speak, but Juliette stopped her advance and pulled the other two girls away from me as well.

"Leave," she said.

My heart, which by this time was already racing, began to beat so hard and so fast I was certain that my shirt was going to flutter from the effort of it. However, I was responding, it was not correct. The drug had been administered and I was immune to it, this was clear. But that they would not continue with their business unless I was fully influenced hardly seemed equitable. "But we are not done here," I protested.

It was to no avail. One of the girls ran out of the room and the other two reached out with cold, clammy hands and firmly gripped me on each side, lifting me off the bed despite my best effort to remain. This I'll attribute also to the drugs I had taken. I have no doubt that under normal circumstances I would not have been so easily overpowered by two frail women. Yet here I was, pulse pounding in my ears at deafening levels, unable to resist their force. They got me out of the room and once I was back in the parlour, Madam DuPont was there to greet me, no doubt summoned by the girl who had left us.

"Perhaps we can try again in a few days," Madam DuPont suggested before I could even utter a sound. The girls began to move me toward the door and I barely heard Madam DuPont answer my query about the prudence of my waiting for Wilkinson so that I could see him safely home. Madam DuPont assured me that Wilkinson would arrive home safely after he had finished his visit and that I had nothing to worry about. All this as the door was slammed in my face for the second time.

I'm beginning to detest this woman.

2 July 1854

Am I hallucinating? This is the question I keep returning to. The stimulating agents I have ingested did not cause hallucinations upon my first trial, but it is possible that my extended exposure to them has altered something in the way my body processes and interacts with them. There is no other explanation I can think of, for what I witnessed through that window sliver this night cannot possibly be real.

I shall endeavour to recount the events as coherently as possible so that once my head is clear I can better determine if these are the ravings of a mad man or if there is a small possibility that what I saw was true.

I returned to Madam DuPont's well after sunset hopeful that no one had noticed that I had pulled apart the curtain. It was not difficult for me to get my bearings and determine to which side of the building I had been taken. There were two windows in close proximity to each other and I was certain the window I sought would be one of these two. I came prepared this time to do a fair amount of paint scraping, knowing full well it might be necessary to remove much of the paint from the window to get the most advantageous view. I set to work on the first window, working slowly so as to not make loud noises which might have been detected from inside. After a few swipes across the entire glass and no sign of light shining through from within, I moved on to the next window. I tried to not allow this wasted effort be a discouragement and began scraping on the second window. Almost immediately I saw a streak of dim light pass through the window and my heart leapt!

I struggled to contain my enthusiasm as I cleared the paint off of the window, carefully to expose as much as needed to get a clear view inside. Once the paint was removed it took some fumbling before I found a comfortable position where I could spy inside. I gave little thought to what a passerby might think of a man lying on his side hugging a building and instead focused on making sure I was comfortable enough to endure the position for hours if necessary. The moon in its new phase only a few nights prior, I hoped the night was still black enough to partially conceal me from any onlookers.

Through the window I could see a fair portion of the room. The edge of the bed and the door were well within my view. As long as the girl was something of a creature of habit, she would escort her next client to the same edge of the bed where she had seated me. If so, my view would be sufficient.

My curiosity was satisfied soon enough when Juliette opened the door and escorted in a man. The man already appeared to be in a state of delirium. Juliette sat him on the edge of the bed, and although I could not hear the conversation, one thing became apparent – Juliette would speak and the man was too far gone to answer. Not even a nod of the head to indicate he had understood he was being spoken to. Juliette smiled at him a few times as she glided across the room and fastened the door closed.

She returned to the bed and pushed the man flat onto his back. She then removed his lower garments, exposing his bottom half. I wanted to turn away, but I felt I was too close to the secret being revealed to me that I forced myself to look. Complicating my view, my own breathing became laboured and as I exhaled the glass on the window would fog over. I dared not wipe the condensation away for fear of making a noise which might alert Juliette to my presence. Instead I began timing my breaths, holding it in as long as I could until I simply could not wait.

I caught only a fleeting glimpse of the man's face as he reclined, and I will classify his expression as one of pure bliss. Whatever Juliette was about to do to him didn't matter. He had already had his money's worth.

What I saw next makes me question my own sanity. Perhaps the awkward body position I had adopted was cutting off blood flow to my brain. Or my stilted deliberate breathing interfered with my senses. But this is what it appeared to me.

Juliette knelt on the floor between the man's legs. With one more smile she tilted her head back and opened her mouth wide revealing extended canines which I swear were not present a moment before. She then plunged her face deep into the man's thigh and when she pulled away, a trickle of blood ran down her chin which she quickly licked away. She reached out and wiped her finger across the man's thigh, then licked her finger. The man's leg, as far as I could see, did not appear to have been cut or gnawed. There was no physical damage visible from this distance. I longed to go examine him in person to see what kind of wound Juliette had inflicted and to determine where the blood had come from.

Then Juliette stood, dressed the man and with an incredible strength, she picked the man up and CARRIED HIM OUT OF THE ROOM! This frail figure lifted a man easily twice her size as if he was nothing more than a pile of clothes.

Once the room was empty, I rolled over onto my back and stared up at the night sky, trying to make sense of what I had seen.

I could not help but recall my nightmare of a few nights prior. Was it truly a nightmare or was it memories of a horrific experience being recalled by my feeble brain which could not make sense of them?

I heard a noise and returned my attention to the window. I watched Juliette as she brought three more men into the room that night. Each one was the same. And which each one I became more convinced that I was not hallucinating.

But now I am not so sure. How is it possible? Are the women in this brothel the result of some unholy union between a man and a cobra? This is the creature she most closely reminded me of prior to her feeding, for that is all I can imagine she was doing. And that is the creature of my nightmare. Or are they some altogether unique species which has been coexisting with humans since the dawn of man? A result of magic? Demons?

Eventually as dawn approached, I knew my night of viewing had to end. I had brought paint with me to cover the window once again, concealing the fact that I had ever been there. If I did not hurry though the first rays of light on this new day would betray me, creeping into the room through curtains which were supposed to be tightly drawn.

2 July 1854

My Dearest Isabel,

Forgive the cryptic nature of this message, but I have no other recourse. There is the possibility that my life may be in danger and I need you to have all relevant information on hand should anything happen to me in the coming days.

I will send you a letter for each day until I have safely departed Japan so that you can rest your mind that my fears have been unjustified. Yet I dare not take a chance. Life is too precious to play with.

Enclosed I have provided a card with the name and address of the woman who I believe will seek my demise in the coming days. I pray that this card is the only encounter you ever have with her.

Lord Wilkinson has informed me that we shall be departing Japan in approximately three days' time and that our return trip will be hasty, his business concluded at all ports. There will be no more sightseeing. We will be of one uniformed intention upon our departure – to make it safely back home.

My journey has been enlightening. I have cases filled with medicinal wonders which I look forward to examining upon my return to England.

I can tell you nothing more at this time, although I long to!

Know that you are in my heart always.

All my love,

Diego

3 July 1854 (later)

Spending a full night is restless wakefulness gives one time to think. To allow a man time to think is a most dangerous thing. When forced to act only on instinct there is no time to plan, to plot, and eventually to second guess. It is live or die, and if you live you are thankful for it. But having time to think, I somehow always can convince myself that the daftest ideas are more plausible than more rational minds would regard them.

A restless night of thought is what led me back to Madam DuPont's. A healthy dose of stimulant is what gave me courage.

With my time in Japan growing short, my resolve to tame the secrets of the venom Madam DuPont and her den of monsters secrete quickly became overwhelming.

To my advantage, Madam DuPont did not know that I was aware of her dark secret. I was able to gain audience with her quickly and she suggested that perhaps I would, on this day, be more receptive to her girls. She apologized for how abruptly my previous visit had ended.

I politely declined and instead asked if we might have a private conference. She was hesitant, but complied and lead me to a private office.

My manner was somewhat threatening, but I thought under the circumstances this would serve me best. Once we were secluded, I immediately informed her that should anything happen to me I had already made arrangements for her business – and perhaps life – to be undone. She smiled several times, waiting for me to enter into the customary euphoria, at which point I bluffed and told her that I was immune to the chemicals in the air. She seemed to believe this, having no choice but to accept the evidence presented.

Her curiosity seemed piqued, and she listened to my entire proposal. At first, she insisted I was mistaken, but after a discourse too lengthy to relate, with me making bold threats which I wasn't sure I could back up, she agreed to comply with my request. Perhaps the knowledge that I would be leaving Japan in a few days gave her some comfort.

I had gone to the place prepared. Madam DuPont had Juliette take me once again into the same, familiar room. Only this time, I opened my doctor's bag and removed Something I had encountered in India — a glass phial with a thin membrane stretched across the top. It was difficult to remind myself that this creature, although resembling a beautiful woman, was not human. The look of mild humiliation on her face as I milked her of her venom did prey on my emotions, but ultimately I allowed the advancement of science to win out.

Madam DuPont has agreed to let me interview the girls and to collect as much venom as I can in the days I have remaining. My bluff proved successful and risking her business seemed something she'd never do. Madam DuPont has also warned that humans have a very low tolerance for the venom, and that my studies of it could be dangerous, or even fatal, if I was not truly immune as I claimed to be.

My part of the bargain... To satisfy Juliette's appetite at each visit. I hope the humiliation on my face spoke to some deep part of her which may be capable of human emotions. We were equal in humiliation. She as I collected a sample and I as she drank from my veins. There is great charity in this venom, making the victim unaware of his status as the next meal. Without its effects, to feel like a piece of meat... There was no pleasure to be had in that room for either of us.

I have filled my first phial with this miracle liquid and the anticipation for my return to England is heightened. Not only will I be reunited with Grace, but I may also have found what I was ultimately seeking on this voyage – the ultimate love potion.

CHAPTER 5 - SPAIN

4 July 1854

My Dearest Isabel,

I regret how I must have frightened you with my last letter. Rest assured that everything has resolved and I no longer believe my life to be in danger.

I'll write more later.

All my love,

Diego

26 April 1854

Querido Diego,

Another new home! How many places you have seen in your life, and here I am living in the shadow of where we were raised.

I worry about you, though. There is a sadness in your letters which I long to help abate. Yet I fully realize that this is something I do not have the power to do.

Life here continues to be a struggle. Antonio does not realize how much pressure he has put me under and when I try to speak to him about it, he tells me I am a silly woman and that I should leave all of the important thinking to him. Still, I am moving through my pregnancy, experiencing new challenges each day which make my old routine difficult to maintain. Antonio takes no sympathy on me. He has made one offer which has had the unfortunate repercussion of making me unwilling to continue the discourse with him – if life is too difficult, his mother can move in with us!

Not that it would be a noticeable difference. She is here all the time, and although she allows Antonio to believe that she assists me with my chores, she does very little in truth. I am still the one who washes the clothes, scrubbing my fingers bare and hurting my back. I am the one who does all the cooking – and not just for the two mouths which I had planned, but for this woman who sits beside her grown male child and still treats him like an infant, wiping crumbs from his face. To make it even more irritating, she can eat more than most men I've ever met! Antonio does not complain about spending extra money for her food, but I would like to use that money to buy some fabric or yarn, to start making some clothes for the baby, rather than stuffing her already plump frame.

I missed you during the Semana Santa processions. Do they celebrate the same way in England as here? You'll have to tell me all about it.

What will I do if she moves in? I can hear you now, counselling me to be tolerant of the old and to humour my husband. Bear this in mind when you do find your love – you are not only marrying the woman. You are marring her entire family. How strange that I never realized this until now. Those warm summer evenings when we were surrounded by two sets of grandparents, cousins from both sides... to children it seemed natural. Family. But our parents did not know these people before they met. They started out as strangers and became so much more. I am just not sure that I will ever be able to have my relationship with Antonio's mother progress the same way. For my child, I must try.

Here I am concerned about your happiness and I spend our time together telling you of my troubles. I pray that your newest home will have an uplifting effect on your spirits and I will make every effort to welcome Antonio's mother into my heart.

Please write again soon.

Besos,

Isabel

2 May 1854

Querido Diego,

I am uncertain of your exact departure date, but perhaps this will find you just prior to your departure.

You must thank the cook for the recipe. I've enclosed one of my favourites in return. Perhaps you might be so kind, if he enjoys this recipe, to ask if we might continue an exchange. Of all of my daily chores, I am finding cooking to be the most pleasurable. I have started a garden. There is great comfort to be found in digging in the dirt, getting Earth under my fingernails. And there is solace. Antonio and his mother do not enjoy being outside!

I do not want to give you a false impression. I do love Antonio, but living together has had some trying moments. He does not value my opinions, so conversation with him is stilted and uncomfortable. As soon as I begin to express an opinion different from his own, he kisses me on the head, calls me a silly woman, and the conversation ends. If a meal has been prepared with too much spice, it is because I am silly. If I did not wash his favourite shirt, it is because I am silly and do not know how to properly manage my time. Yet he does not ever disagree with anything his mother says.

I hope that your new family in England is nice. Perhaps you will finally meet someone who is worth cultivating a relationship with. I know it has been difficult for you to meet people and make friends your entire life – although I do not know why. You are such a smart, interesting man. And I do not only say this to you from sisterly love.

Drawing again! I am so pleased for you. You always had so much talent at it that I was sad when you stopped before.

It sounds like this Lord Wilkinson is a perfect match for you. A job where you will be able to travel? I can think of nothing which would suit you more. Please do send me detailed accounts of your travels. Places and people I will never see...

Besos,

Isabel

3 August 1854

My dearest Isabel,

Do you remember when we would spend warm summer evenings visiting with our grandmother? She had that crooked tree behind her house which was the perfect shape for climbing. Her house was small and we would all pile into the bed together, throwing the covers off because it was far to humid to be covered even to sleep? We slept, but it was not the same as sleeping at home. If you awoke in the night there was a moment of confusion as you wondered where you were and you had to reorient yourself to your surroundings. The sounds of the morning and the way the light filtered in through the windows was all different, all new.

I started to read some of your letters. I am sorry that I have not written for a while. If you haven't yet deduced, I have finally returned to England. I have secluded myself from Lord Wilkinson and his family, understandably seeking some time to myself after having spent so much time in his close companionship.

A most unusual sight greeted me upon my return to my small cottage. Although I had the place closed up tightly for my departure, somehow a swarm of bees managed to find an ingress, but once inside, they could not discover their narrow channel to once again gain their freedom. The result being that they all eventually wore themselves out and this swarm of dead bees covered the floor. I have collected them – ever the scientist – and perhaps I will one day make use of them. I retain some fear that a second swarm may discover this same route while I occupy the space. Can you imagine waking up with a swarm of bees surrounding you in your bedroom? An event we can only hope to never experience.

Seeing England again has been a welcome reward. The nights away were somewhat like the nights we spent at our grandmothers? I was not alone, so I did not feel the same isolation (and adventure) which I have felt before when traveling. Instead I felt like I was in a strange place, but not entirely away from home. The ship became much like a home. Lord Wilkinson was determined to make our return trip as quick as possible. The ship pulled into ports only long enough to freshen supplies and exchange crew. Sometimes we were only docked for an hour before we set out again. Little concern was given to ocean conditions. We pressed on day and night. Although the return trip was lacking in adventure, the anticipation of returning to England sustained us through the long nights.

I have collected so many specimens during my travels! Now I must settle down to the hard work of examining what I have collected to determine if anything has any actual value.

Perhaps I am mistaken, but I do believe that I have found what I had hoped to on my journey. It is still premature to give you the details, dear sister, but very soon I hope to be able to share my discovery with you.

But you must tell me, how is your pregnancy progressing? When is the baby due? Perhaps I will find further illumination on the subject as I continue reading your letters, but I do think about you and the baby often and am desperate for an update! Just writing about it now ignites a fire within me to tear through your remaining letters to learn of your news. You see, your brother has not learned patience in his travels.

Did I tell you that I stood on a mountain near the African shore and looked out across the water toward home? I imagined that I could see you standing on the far side, waving and smiling at me. I must have told you...

Ah, now to reading and resting and tomorrow I will tackle new problems and come up with new solutions.

All my love,

Diego

2 May 1854

Querido Diego,

I cannot wait to see your sketches. Perhaps you will one day teach my child how to draw.

I get ahead of myself. Sorry. I know I must seem somewhat disoriented, but I spend so much of my time imagining what the future will be like as a family. Will this child be the first of many? Will Antonio's mother become my ally once the baby is born? Will it be a boy or a girl? Taking after Antonio, or will some of your qualities find their way through me to the child?

I had a nightmare last night that Antonio's mother, Valentina, waited until I slept and stole the baby away in the night. In the dream, morning came and I was all alone, Antonio having gone back to his mother to raise our child with her.

I know I should tell you happier news, but there is no happy news to tell aside from my child. Valentina has moved in with us and although the guise is that she is making life easier for me during my pregnancy, in truth she does nothing when Antonio is not around. And when he is around, she talks bad about me to him. She is driving a wedge between us, and I fear that Antonio is too easily swayed by her to protest as she works to tear us apart. When I disagree with her, she just tells him, "See how she is? When you aren't here, she argues with me nonstop."

But I am glad to read that you have made some friends on your journey. It is good that you do not isolate yourself with Lord Wilkinson and that you have taken the initiative to explore your new surroundings!

I very much enjoyed reading your story about the chameleon. I started to remember the stories we told each other as children about the animals of our own homeland.

Do you remember the story of the flamingo? Two lovers were separated by a war and the man, as he lay dying in the battlefield encountered a flamingo. The flamingo was all white. As the man told the flamingo of his love and how he fought to keep her safe, rain began to fall. The rain hit the blood-soaked ground, splashing onto the flamingo. Touched by the man's story, the bird refused to wash off the blood so that me might serve as a visual reminder of dedication to love and country.

The flamingo went in search of the woman to tell her that the man had died bravely in battle. When he found her, she was so distraught she cried for days. The flamingo stayed by her side, never once leaving, with only her tears to drink. After that, the bird determined to always live in salty water to remind him of the woman's love for the man.

I need to work on my storytelling so that when my child is old enough to hear these stories, I might be able to tell them eloquently. Yes, I will save your letters – I look forward to more stories – so that at least some of the stories I can read and not have to rely on my own memory and tongue.

Besos,

Isabel

4 August 1854 (Diego's Diary)

I thought that once I had returned to England, some of the discontent I have been suffering from would evaporate. As if the air here would suddenly cure me of my ills.

I have not seen Grace since returning. From what I hear, she has been spending most of her time with David. Wilkinson has called for a big family dinner, to which I have been invited, to take place in a few nights' time, so I am certain I will see Grace then. And in the meantime, I must do everything I can to make progress on distilling the vital elements of the items I have brought back with me from my voyage.

I have enlisted the cook's help in capturing mice and rats on which I can test the qualities of the various substances I brought here to study. Since I gave her Isabel's recipe in return for her own, the two of them have begun their own correspondence and this has helped warm the cook's heart toward me. Thanks to my sister, I have one solid ally in this house of strangers.

The cottage is not ideal as a laboratory, but for now it will need to do. Wilkinson has offered that I might clear out a stable for extra space to work, but here in the cottage I have a stove and privacy – two things which I desperately need while conducting my experiments.

But to get back to Grace. The thought of seeing her again was one of the only things which sustained me during my travels. Now, knowing that she has used my time away to grow closer to another man, the one person who brings me the most joy in the world is also causing me endless grief.

Is this the way of all love? The stories of youth told of seeing a woman and in a flash you both know that you are meant to be together always and forever. An unspoken bond which lasts through eternity is created the instant your eyes meet. How long must a man wait for this experience? Am I in the midst of a false start or is not how love works? Are these stories romanticized to fool youth into acting out on fleeting emotions? A trick of the older generation.

My parents are not happy. That is not to say that they are unhappy. It is just that even though I can look at them each in turn and imagine what they may have been like in their youth, I cannot imagine that they ever partook of the joyous romping which I so long to share with Grace. There is no spark behind their eyes when they look at each other. And an ember such as I've been taught must exist could not be squelched, not even by such an enemy as time.

What is it? Why does my heart ache so? Why do I secretly desire that Grace and David should have a falling out? Is there some chance that David is a better match for her? I have not seen them together, but perhaps she has that fire in her eyes when she looks at him and he at her. How, in a just world, could this be? I do want her to be happy, yet I cannot find a resolution in my mind between the ideas that she should be happy and that she could be happy without me. I cannot fathom being happy without her.

And so, I am confronted with this harsh reality that love is not the love I have been taught. There is no magical moment which we shared when we first cast eyes on each other. It is a moment I shall remember until the day I die, which I suspect Grace could not recall if given that same amount of time to do so. What is the answer? Is she wooable? Can a person be influenced to love?

If I measure each word carefully, comb my hair just so, can I somehow become a man she will take note of? Will one of the items I have brought back from my journey help sway her mind and emotions – and if it can, is that something I can be content with? If she loves me, but not of her own free will, is there value in the love or will I still suffer this oppressive sorrow knowing that her feelings, on some fundamental level, are false.

Can I be loved?

1 June 1854

Querido Diego,

My heart leapt when I received your last letter. To see your drawings! I could not believe my eyes. You have always been so talented, brother, and to see that time has not robbed you of this gift made me so happy. I was equally enchanted by the content of the drawings. Did you really see a giant cat with a woman's face? There are so many things in this world which I cannot even begin to imagine. And the pyramids! How large are they? Oh, you must give me more details!

I am sorry to hear that you are lonely. Although my life with Antonio has not been as I dreamed it would, I am never alone. I think part of the comfort of being married comes not from finding your other half, not from having someone you love in your life, but in not being alone. Knowing that if you want to go for a walk there is someone to ask to go with you. As simple as that! No more walks on your own. But you must consider equally that there are no more evenings on your own. No more quiet enjoyment of a sunset on your own. How I long for just one night to be able to retire when I am ready without having to either wait for Antonio to be ready for sleep or being told I must go to sleep well before I have tired because it is improper for a husband and wife to keep different schedules.

Valentina living here further complicates my ability to be alone. Every move I make is watched to the extent that to write to you I must wait until both Valentina and Antonio are occupied with their own interests. Valentina has made some friends with the other old women in the village and goes to visit them at least once a week to gossip. So far, I have not been forced to accompany her. And Antonio, doting on the baby, not me, can be turned away from the house by my asking him for some favour "for the baby" during those times when Valentina is gone. Even if I just ask him to go pick some fresh herbs from the garden, it gives me those few moments alone which are so dear to me now.

I cannot simply say that I have a desire for a moment's privacy to compose a letter to my brother as that only leads to a seemingly endless stream of questions from them both. What are you writing to him about? Where is he living now? Has he married yet? Does he have any plans to visit? Have you considered visiting him, because you know now that the baby is coming it will be nearly impossible? Can you include a note to ask him about the sore on my toe? And, why do you write to him so often?

Harmless, I'm sure, but I cannot help but feel that underlying these questions is a desire to control me. And the questions do not stop at your letters. Each time I stand I am asked by one or the other why I have stood. Do I plan on going somewhere? Each time I make a noise I am asked why. Is the baby moving? Am I comfortable? Do I need something to eat? Would I like another pillow? Because if that's why I have stood up, to get another pillow, I should have just asked!

The questioning and the watching begins as soon as I wake up in the morning, and because Antonio insists we retire at the same time, it doesn't seem to end. It is only in sleep that I find any solitude.

When the baby comes, I think they will both divert their attention away from me and on to the baby so by then perhaps I will be able to catch my breath. You cannot imagine how ill at ease a person becomes knowing that they are being watched every waking moment!

My advice to you is to treasure this time you have alone. Perhaps your life will not mirror mine once you are married, but if it does, you will look back on your lost freedom fondly. See? I'm already preparing for motherhood – giving out unwanted advice!

Besos,

Isabel

10 June 1854

Querido Diego,

I must confess that I was saddened when I read your last letter, dear brother. Written only a few short days later, and yet your mood so suddenly dark. You did mention that you were feeling lonely, but I had no idea of the extent. Did something happen on your journey which you are keeping from me?

I will tell you, because you have asked, that I do not consider Antonio to be my other half. Perhaps when we first met, I was blinded by a youthful innocence which created the illusion that he was something other than what he is. It is only now, after having lived with him for some time, that I truly feel like I know this man. And had I known him before, I am not so certain I would have chosen him as my life partner.

I honestly say that we do not fight. This is only because I lack the passion to engage him when he is cruel to me. Instead, I accept it and the veil which covers my eyes is drawn back even further. He is cruel in so many little ways that I doubt he realizes how he behaves. Yesterday, as an example, we had bread and butter with our dinner. Many times, I will mix herbs and garlic in the butter to add more flavour, but yesterday I was feeling unwell because of my pregnancy and I allowed Valentina to prepare the meal. Antonio, upon noticing that the butter was plain decided to call me stupid and took my hand and smeared it with butter. When I tried to stand to go clean myself, he refused to allow it, holding me down so that I would finish the meal with butter on my hand. Valentina did not come to my defence, instead she agreed with Antonio that I was stupid, adding that I was also lazy and that was why the meal was inferior this evening.

So, no. I do not lay in bed at night and look upon the face of my love, feeling confident that together there is nothing we cannot overcome. Instead I look upon his face and worry that our child will learn from his father these behaviours and be disrespectful to me and to others.

If I cannot provide my child with a better start, a stronger mind, the benefit of my own experiences and wisdom, then I have failed as a mother.

Our mother used to tell us stories about love. How two people would see each other and know in their hearts immediately that there was no other person better suited for them anywhere on Earth. She would talk about princesses being rescued by princes they had never before met, and yet somehow going on to live their lives together in perfect bliss. I look at Antonio and I realize that these stories were nothing but lies. But thinking about my own child, they are lies I will continue to tell. I want my child to grow up believing that there is such a thing as a perfect love. To seek it. Because if my child doesn't know to seek it, he will settle for whatever comes along and improve his chances of never truly being happy. I still believe such a thing exists, even though I did not manage to find it.

Perhaps you will be able to share this perfect love with someone one day. I will wish this for you.

Besos,

Isabel

12 August 1854

Most of my preliminary studies on many of the substances I brought back from my journey have proved disappointing. One substance said to convey invisibility instead caused temporary blindness in my rat subjects. Thankfully it did prove to be temporary! Others have caused such undesirable observable effects as loss of motor function, uncontrollable salivation, increased appetite, increased thirst and lethargy. If these rats could speak, I imagine they would report even greater detrimental effects.

However, two substances are showing some promise. The first is an herb from the African desert which appears to completely numb an area once applied. I have yet to determine if this numbing effect has any lingering negative results, but if it does not then this could be a highly beneficial substance bringing relief to injuries and dulling the skin to allow for minor surgical procedures.

The other substance which shows promise is my collection from Madam DuPont's. My elixir. I have diluted it 1-part elixir to 1000 parts water for my first bout of testing. My research on the elixir is focused on two elements. First, to determine the full extent of the wonders of this substance. Second, to determine what the detrimental effect of long-term exposure might be. Madam DuPont was adamant about not allowing any of her clients to be exposed to the substance for more than a few hours a week, so it stands to reason that in small doses it is beneficial, in large doses it is quite the opposite.

I have two test groups. The first has controlled quantities of the elixir for limited durations each week. I will study them for immediate effects. The second test group has the elixir mixed into their drinking water at all times.

The tremendous temptation in this, which I struggle to overcome each day, is to confine my experiments to the rats and to not partake of the elixir myself. The limited quantity of elixir which I have helps to control my urge. If I were to even dip a finger in to taste, I would be using up my most precious commodity. I fear that one day the desire to lose myself in that world of endless bliss will be too much to resist.

24 July 1854

Querido Diego,

You know that were I a man I would already be at your side! Your last letter terrified me so! It is only because of my current state that I did not rush out of the house as soon as I started reading it to seek passage across the sea. I know not where you are, yet I would have taken my chances and set out hoping that fate would safely guide me to your side. With only the address of your potential murderess, it would be a foolish journey indeed.

Are you even reading this? This is a question I often ask myself. There have been no other incidents when I wondered if the reason you might not read it is because you have been the victim of foul play, though.

Writing a letter can never compare to speaking with you in person, but perhaps this is the only way you and I will ever after communicate. I read and re-read every word you write to me.

Now I fear I will not be able to sleep, staying awake with worry all night that another letter will not arrive. What kind of dangerous people are you meeting in your travels? I had no idea that being a personal physician involved so much risk, otherwise I would have counselled you against taking the position.

What happens if a letter does not arrive tomorrow? A second restless night followed by a third? If any of the herbs and potions you study upon your return aid in sleep or in calming nerves, you will have to be sure to forward them to me. For now, I'll see if I can find some of the herbal folk remedies our mother was so fond of to help soothe my spirit. Lavender, chamomile, milk: these are the only remedies I have at my disposal. I pray that they will be enough.

Why do you terrify me so? I will pray that you are safe and that I hear from you with haste.

Besos,

Isabel

26 July 1854

Querido Diego,

Why have you put me through this! At least I am happy that you are still alive. I received two letters from you today. I can only hope that you leave that strange land soon so that we can both stop worrying about your welfare.

The past two days have been troublesome for many reasons. Antonio was aware that something was on my mind, and rather than ask me what my concern was (although I wonder if I would have told him the truth), he decided to search through the house looking for clues as to what might be bothering me. I am not certain what kind of clues he hoped to find, but what he did find was my box of your letters.

It is not a secret to him that I keep in touch with you, but I do my best to keep him from seeing the letters. If he does see me with one and asks, I tell him only the most basic information of your life. But for him to find them, and to see that they are written in English so that he could not read them, he became enraged. He has convinced himself that these letters are not from you, because he doesn't understand why I would speak to my own brother in a foreign tongue. He believes I am corresponding with another man and that our relationship is in jeopardy.

We argued for what seemed like hours, with Valentina watching the whole exchange. Although I do not appreciate her being a spectator of a private matter, I have no doubt that her presence prevented Antonio from being violent with me. He raised his hand a few times as if to strike, but then caught his mother's eye and stepped away.

My baby will be born soon, and I have decided to stay with our own parents for a while to have the baby and to allow Antonio to regain some perspective on our relationship. And so that I may clear my head. Mother will be pleased. I only hope that I am still able to travel home. Although it is a short distance, even walking outside of our house and not being able to sit for a few minutes can be taxing.

If I stay here, I know that Antonio's watch on me will only increase. What little privacy I have is about to be restricted at a time when I feel I desperately need it.

I will wait a few days before leaving, to hopefully receive a letter that you have left Japan and are on your way back to England safely.

I pray that you return to England soon.

Besos,

Isabel

CHAPTER 6 - SELF

17 August 1854

I have placed the studies of all other substances I brought back with me from my trip on hold so that I may concentrate my efforts on the study of the elixir.

Sharing my cottage with dozens of nocturnal beings proved to be a mistake. While I wanted to sleep, the rats stayed up all night and did their very best to ensure that I was aware of their every move. As a scientist, there may have been some value in this, but as a human, I needed sleep to be able to function during the day. The rats had to go.

Wilkinson was kind enough to allow me the use of a small outbuilding. The main drawback is that it is on the outskirts of the property so I am isolated from all activities in the house when I retire to the lab. I must also ensure that the staff in the house are all well aware of my whereabouts in case I am required for a medical situation at the main house. This has restricted the amount of time I am able to spend studying the rats, but in the long term I think it is for the best. A physician who is sleep deprived is worse than one who cannot be immediately located.

Dead rats are still welcomed in my cottage. Once they have served their usefulness in live study and it becomes time to dissect them, I can bring their little lifeless bodies back to my cottage for the post-mortem examination.

The rats which have been taking the elixir in small, controlled quantities do not, so far, appear to be undergoing any lasting changes in their physiques or personalities. They appear to enter into a temporary delirium shortly after exposure, not wanting to eat or drink. Once the elixir is out of their systems, they return to their usual habits and seem none the worse for wear.

The rats which have been taking the elixir as part of their regular drinking water exhibited the same delirium when their exposure first began, and it was sustained for approximately seventy-two hours before a short period when they appeared to be completely immune to the elixir. After that, they have the most miraculous improvements in overall health. Their strength and stamina increased. Any blemishes or injuries heal with remarkable speed. But their aggression has increased. It has been more than one morning when I have entered the lab to see one rat has been viciously murdered by his companions. In the mornings, though, the rats seem calm and tired. Their level of activity increases dramatically at nightfall.

Are these two groups heading down the same path at different rates or are they on different paths? I suppose that is what I am trying to determine. My question with the rats in the controlled quantity group is if they will eventually begin to exhibit the same traits as the other group and if it is only because of the limited exposure that they are progressing slowly.

I question my own willpower in this endeavour. How long will I be content studying these effects in rats before I long for a human subject? Each time I measure out the elixir for these creatures, I remember how it felt to partake of it myself and the temptation to do so again is getting harder and harder to resist. My supply of the drug is dwindling, and each drop which I feed to a rat is one drop which will not be available for a real breakthrough. A human breakthrough.

I dread the idea, but perhaps Wilkinson knows of another such brothel in Paris or London where I might be able to replenish my supply. How dare I ask him such a thing?

How dare I not?

20 August 1854

I was late getting out to my lab this morning, and I must only credit God with my delay.

Cook informed me last evening that her traps were once again full and that I should come and collect the rats to remove them from her kitchen. I was not able to visit her last night, and so I had to go this morning. When I returned from the kitchen with the cages in tow, I noticed fair Grace seated in the arbour, distraught.

Not wishing to approach her with vermin, I hastened to my cottage to deposit the rats for later retrieval. I then flew to Grace's side to comfort her.

She had an argument with David the day prior and had lost all faith in love. Despite my overwhelming desire to convince her that she was better off without David and that it was, perhaps, for the best that she realise now, while their relationship was still new, that he is not the right man for her, I was not given the chance. Until this moment I had been unaware that in addition to Grace's beauty, she possesses an almost inhuman ability to talk. I sat with her for most of the morning, and the most I was ever able to utter was an occasional "Mm," or "Yes—" before I was cut off again by her continuing story.

In retrospect, it was best that I was unable to speak. If I had been given the opportunity, I am sure I would have declared my undying love for her, and even I realize it is the wrong time. By my forced silence, I was able to become her confidant and preserve the hope of a successful future for us together.

By luncheon, Grace was feeling better for having talked out her troubles, and I was much delayed in my research. I returned to the cottage, collected my rats, and headed out to my lab.

Before I had made it there, I could smell the smoke in the air. It didn't register with me immediately what the smoke might be from, but as I got closer to the lab, the smell got stronger, and the air became thick with ash. I could hear the rumbling of the flames and the truth became undeniable. All of my work since returning from my trip was going up in flames.

Had I gotten there earlier, perhaps I could have prevented the fire, or perhaps I would have been trapped inside, dying now with all of my research. I can only assume that it is for the best that this has happened, but the idea of this is in conflict with my own baser emotions.

How much of my elixir is gone now? Wasted! With the quantity I have left in my cottage, I must now decide if I start my experiments over with rats or formulate a new plan.

I set the newly captured rats free. Those that died in the fire, no benefit has come from their deaths. No lessons have been learned. Setting their family free to live another day and perhaps avoid the trap the next time is the least I could do for them.

24 August 1854

I write this entry from London. After the accident at my lab, I understandably was shaken and Wilkinson thought it would be best if I accompany him to London for a few days. He is here for legitimate business, so I am free to spend my days how I want. His only requirement is that I not miss the train when it is time to return to his estate. The time away from him, in the city again, will do me some good.

I visited Mary and Thomas today. It seems like a lifetime since I saw them last. I told them all about my travels and my research. They seemed interested to know if I found anything to help them with their condition. I did present them with a gift – an African fertility idol. We shared a good laugh about it, but as I left, I think we all had the same feeling, that it just might work.

It felt good to stretch my legs and roam down familiar streets again. It was almost as if I was seeing London for the first time, through new eyes, having been away for what seems like a lifetime. I turned down streets I had been down thousands of times before, and yet they seemed so new. I suppose it is inevitable that the city, like a living, breathing entity, would change. Businesses I used to frequent had closed up and new ones had sprung up in their place.

I roamed back to my own little shop and was surprised to see that it had not been leant to another physician, but that a perfumery was now located there. My own curiosity to see this old familiar place got the better of me and in I went. The man who owned the shop, a burly Frenchman (who I dare say could have sampled his own wares more frequently), was extremely pleasant and we had a good conversation. He showed me his favourite fragrances and urged me to make a purchase.

Just as I was about to leave, not having bought a thing, an idea sprang to mind. I wondered if perhaps I might not have use of one of his atomizers in my study of the elixir – it would make a wonderful distribution method, very similar to the method Madam DuPont and her women employed. I turned around just as my hand was upon the front door and inquired if I might be able to purchase several empty bottles.

I wasn't thinking! His face became so long, believing I did not appreciate his talent and that I was mocking him somehow. Seeing no way to elegantly explain my plans to him, I decided that purchasing the perfume was the best plan. So once again, he showed me all of the fragrances he had created and implored me to choose my favourite. It was at this time I discovered something previously unknown about myself – I don't like the smell of perfume. They were all so heavy and spicy and mysterious. I asked him if he had something crisper, and the result was the two of us spending more time than I had planned inventing a new perfume together. Something made from almonds and lemons and oranges. Light and fruity and sweet.

He filled four of his finest atomizers with our new concoction and we parted ways – him much happier for my having stopped in, me much poorer for doing so!

Four bottles, though, is more than I need of a perfume I didn't want in the first place. Perhaps I will offer one to Grace.

I also spent some time today sketching in the park. I am on a break from life. No experiments, no doctoring, no work, no schedules, no boat to meet or camel to ride. If only my life could always be so carefree.

25 August 1854

I had to meet Wilkinson late this morning to catch the train back to the country, but before meeting up with him I decided to try my luck with a visit to Felicity. She refused to open the door to me, instead screaming profanities through the walls, loud enough that I'm sure people could hear them several houses down. This poor woman! If I had had some elixir with me, I would have spared a drop to help bring her at least one moment's comfort.

On the train I spent a good deal of time considering how to best incorporate the elixir with my new delivery method of perfume bottles.

Things which I do not yet have the answer to:

Does the elixir only work when ingested (sniffed or drank) or is it also effective when applied directly to the skin?

Diluting the elixir with water did not seem to weaken its effectiveness, can the same be said of other liquids like alcohol or an alcohol based perfume?

If mixed with one of the perfumes, will the elixir remain effective as long as the perfume does? So that if one were to wear the perfume, say on their wrist, and not feel the effects of the elixir through direct skin contact, could they offer said wrist to others to smell? Would they then be able to administer the drug for the duration of the scent on their wrist, provided they themselves avoided smelling it?

Once airborne in such a manner, would the elixir lose potency as it travelled through the air, being strongest when inhaled directly from the wrist and least potent if only a whiff of scent was caught on a passing breeze?

But all of my thoughts brought me back to the same methodology – shifting my experiments from rats to humans. And if I were to experiment on humans, would I be the main test subject, would I seek volunteers, or would I introduce the substance secretly and record the results through observation?

Inherently the elixir has already proven to be quite safe if the quantity is controlled, despite the dire warnings. Perhaps I should use rats to test exactly what happens when proportionally massive quantities are ingested.

Even as I write that suggestion to myself, I cringe at the thought of wasting time with rats and shudder even more at the idea of my dwindling supply! I must consider this matter carefully before proceeding.

27 August 1854

My Dearest Isabel,

If you are reading this it means that either you have moved home and are spending the last few weeks of your pregnancy with our mother, or she has forwarded it on to you. I took my chances in sending it to her that you were more likely to receive it this way than if I sent it to Antonio.

Not that I wish to speak ill of your husband, but your letters have certainly not endeared him to me. I wonder how it will be the next time I see him, knowing that he is not as gentlemanly with you as he should be. I pray I can hold my tongue, for your sake.

Now that distance and time have cleared my head, I realize it was foolish of me to worry you so. I can scarcely remember how distraught I must have been to believe I needed to take such dramatic measures. All is well now and I will try not to distress you again as it cannot be good for you or your child to suffer such intense emotions.

How amazing it is that an emotion can feel so intense one moment and can be nearly forgotten the next. At least, for me, this is the case with emotions such as anger and fear. I seem to be quite the opposite when it comes to love. Time has no effect on how intensely I experience love. I wonder if I am alone in this. Do some people hold tightly to the negative emotions and allow the wondrous ones to slip away? I hope that you, dear sister, hold love tightly and allow hatred and resentment to only hold you in fleeting moments.

Perhaps once your child arrives you and Antonio will be able to recapture the spirit of love that existed when your relationship was new. And perhaps Valentina will soften to you, too. Of course, I will only wish this for you if it is what you desire. I do not want my wishes for you to be contrary to your own.

How easy it is to look at the life of another and make judgments about what is or is not best for them, yet seemingly impossible to look at our own lives with this same objectivity. Only you know what is best for you, and I will do my best to support you in whatever decision you make. If you decide to live with our parents for a long time, I will not let this be a barrier to our own relationship. How horrible that sounds of me! I am aware that it is not a pleasant thing to say, but I thought it might ease your mind to know that I do not begrudge your relationship with our mother.

Life back in England has been a welcomed relief, although it has not been idyllic. I did have a wonderful conversation with Grace the other day, and I am happy to be involved in my research. I am impatient on both fronts for faster results. I am tested every day.

I hope that soon I will have more interesting news to tell you. Perhaps once I am farther along in my experiments, I will.

You must let me know how soon it is until you are due exactly so that I can try and schedule some time off to come and visit you. Until then, I will hold a good thought for you that things will work out how you desire so that you can be happy.

All my love,

Diego

27 August 1854

Dear Madam DuPont,

I can only imagine how surprised you must be to receive a letter from me! First let me set your mind at ease that I have no intention of betraying your secret and there is nothing sinister in my contacting you.

I had the opportunity to speak at some length with my traveling companion, Lord Wilkinson, during our long journey back to our own tiny island after leaving the one which you now call home. He informed me that, although he did not know the full story of how you came to live in Japan, so far from Paris where you were raised, he did know that part of the reason you had decided to strike out for new adventures was because of a row you had with your sister. I can only imagine that it must certainly have been a vicious fight with bad feelings all around to drive you from your home into a foreign land.

Perhaps somewhere deep inside you still stoke a fire of resentment or hatred against her? Not that I wish to drudge up bad memories, but would you, perhaps, receive some pleasure in setting someone such as myself upon her?

But I make one leap in my logic. I am assuming that your own special physique is something which your sister might share. Perhaps she is even in the same profession as you, still in Paris?

I suffered a setback in my research and I desperately require an additional supply of that which only you and your staff can provide me. Unless you might help me locate another source. If you have forgiven your sister with time, then I can only imagine you are laughing as you read this – having no pity for the man who got the better of you, if only briefly. But if you still feel the same rage which you once did, then please allow me to help you exact some revenge by being a thorn in your sister's side, instead of yours.

You must be able to sense my desperation in contacting you this way. I wouldn't be doing it if I didn't think there was tremendous value to all of mankind in your unique fluids.

Please do not try and send someone to hunt me down to exact your revenge upon me as it would prove more difficult that you anticipate. The address I have provided is not my own but that of an unwitting accomplice who does not yet even know of his involvement in my scheme. Sending someone to him would yield nothing he doesn't even know my name, let alone how to find me. And as I said, I do not wish to cause you any undo trouble. I am simply imploring upon your better nature to aid in scientific progress. You have already contributed what may become one of the greatest substances known to man, all I'm asking is for your help in procuring an additional supply so that my research can continue.

Fondly,

Diego Amador

3 September 1854

With my remaining supply of elixir, I am concentrating my efforts on determining the compounds which make it up rather than continuing to study the effects. If I am unable to obtain an additional supply, my only hope of continuing my research will be if I am able to synthesize my own version of it.

I have taken one phial and set it up to evaporate off any liquid compound and leave any solids. Could it be a salt contained within the liquid which causes the effects? Is it the liquid? Until I know which part of the substance causes the miraculous effects, I cannot begin to effectively endeavour to recreate it. I do not want my labour to be wasted. Perhaps the liquid is nothing more than regular water? Saliva? Nothing unique. Or perhaps there is something in the makeup of the liquid itself which needs to be studied.

The liquid is collected in a new phial from the vapor condensing. The process has farther reduced my overall supply as I was not able to collect all of the evaporating liquid and some of it did manage to escape into the air.

The first observation I was able to make was that the liquid did not evaporate of its own accord. I set up my contraption and waited for two days for the liquid to travel from the dish to the collection phial without any movement. It was then that I determined I would need to subject the liquid to a high temperature, to boil it, to induce evaporation. This was successful.

The second observation was that the liquid I ended up with after the separation was photo-sensitive. I held the phial up to the window to see the clarity of it in the sunlight and it began to smoulder. I quickly brought it back inside my dim cottage and the smouldering subsided. I then decided it was worth a sacrifice of one drop and daubed it on a piece of paper which I brought out into the full sun. The paper caught fire as soon as a clear ray of sun was cast upon it. I repeated the experiment with a drop of the unfiltered elixir and the result was similar, although the paper took much longer – by several minutes – to catch fire.

Could I have unwittingly caused that fire in my lab? I never imagined that the elixir would not be able to withstand something as simple as sunlight. Thinking back over my supply and the journey it took from Japan to here, I realized that it wasn't until this day that I had exposed any of it to direct sun. It had certainly seen many rays of indirect sun and candlelight, as I was not carrying out my experiments in the dark. But it was collected in Madam DuPont's establishment where all of the windows were covered, carried in my pockets or bag back to my room, transported on the ship in my luggage, and then only removed from my luggage once I was back inside my cottage. Even when I transported the rats from my cottage to the lab, once the experiment had begun, I took care to cover their cages so they would not be overly agitated by being moved.

I took another drop of the highly concentrated liquid and dampened a piece of paper. This one I kept inside in a dish just out of the sun's rays. For the entire day it did not ignite. Direct sun only causes this caustic reaction. And one more of my questions was answered – this liquid certainly isn't water or saliva.

To first determine if some chemical reaction may have occurred during the separation of the elements which may have rendered either the liquid or the salts toxic, I have once again resorted to my faithful rats to assist me in my research. I gave one cage of rats a diluted solution of the liquid and the other cage of rats received the salts mixed with water. The salt group is exhibiting behaviours most similar to those which were given the elixir in original form, yet I am now at a disadvantage. Those who have taken only the liquid do not appear to be having any effects at all. Also concerned that ingesting this highly flammable liquid may render the rats (and by extrapolation, an eventual human subject) likewise flammable, I have selected one rat as a possible sacrifice and set him in a cage by himself in the sun.

I knew firsthand the effects of the elixir, but these new substances may not be causing the same reaction. By tomorrow I will be satisfied that the rats did not die from ingesting the new substances and I will do that which all good scientists must refrain from doing at all costs – I shall experiment on myself.

Keeping in mind Madam DuPont's warning, I believe I will be safe enough if I only test on myself once per week. If the rat bursts into flame over the course of the day, I am not sure I will have the courage to test the liquid. Only time will tell if my rats satisfy my curiosity and prove that, if nothing else, the new substances I have created are not fatal.

4 September 1854

The rats are all still alive. No deaths in either group, and the one which I set outside did not ignite, so I felt it was safe enough to proceed with a test upon myself.

I felt absolutely giddy as I prepared a sample of the liquid. It is at times like this, when my excitement becomes so undeniable, that I wonder if I am not undergoing all of my experiments for the sole purpose of enhancing my own pleasure. I prefer to believe that I have more altruistic motives and that the elixir will benefit all of mankind once I am able to unlock its secrets...if I can overcome my own greed and share it with the world.

I felt confident that one solid drop of elixir placed on my tongue would be sufficient to fully experience any effects of this newly created liquid.

As I had observed in the rats, the liquid did not retain the euphoria-inducing abilities of the unaltered venom. I waited in my lab for approximately one hour, hoping to experience some marked effect, yet none came that I could perceive. I decided to go for a walk on the grounds.

Once I had left the confines of my lab, I was astounded by the effects of the drug. As I strolled toward the house, I saw Grace and her sister Rosemary just leaving. Though I must have been hundreds of yards away from them, I could see them quite clearly. I saw that Rosemary carried a small basket with her, going out to collect flowers from the garden. She had decided not to wear gloves and wondered if perhaps she shouldn't go back inside and get some before handling the plants. I saw that Grace had a blue ribbon in her hair and that one tail on it was longer than the other. Even as I took note of these things, I realized that the details I was seeing were so clear that it was almost as if I was standing right next to them. I could see a strand of hair as it was caught by a passing breeze and dropped in front of Grace's eye and watched as she brushed it away with her hand.

I stopped walking and not only was I watching the sisters, but to my astonishment I was also listening to them. Rosemary told Grace that she couldn't find her gloves and hoped that she would not prick her finger on any thorns. Rosemary then asked Grace how David was and when he would be coming back. I immediately felt a twinge of guilt for eavesdropping on this private conversation, and resumed my walk, hoping that by moving I would draw attention to myself. They did take note of my arrival, but it only served to steer the conversation away from David and on to me. Rosemary admitted to Grace that she had a bit of a crush on me. I was flattered, but the affection of a child is not something I seek. Grace looked over at me and I gave a polite wave. She then asked Rosemary if she didn't think I was too old. Too old? Me? The very thought of it made my heart sink and I stopped listening to their conversation as I felt the blood rush through my veins. All other sounds died down and the only sound I could hear was of a beating heart. At first, I thought it was my own, but then I realized it was Grace's.

I began to feel giddy realizing the effects of this new drug. My senses were heightened to such an extent as I could not have imagined. I headed to the kitchen to see if my senses of taste and smell were equally as heightened, listening to the sounds along the way. Crickets walking through the grass. A cat a mile away squealing with delight as it cornered a mouse. The breeze down the road kissing the leaves so that I knew precisely the moment it would likewise kiss my own cheek.

My sense of smell was heightened, I realized along the way. I could smell the fear of the cornered mouse – yes, the fear had an odour which I had never perceived before. I could smell the flowers which Rosemary intended to cut. I could smell a burst of fresh grass beneath my feet as each step caused the slender stalks to yield. And my sense of touch was also put to the test on this walk. I felt the delicate beating of mosquito wings near my arm and knew in an instant the size and location of the insect without even looking over at it. I could feel rumbling through the earth the footsteps of everyone in the house. I knew exactly which room each person was in, recognizing them by their weight and bearing. My hairs stood on end and alerted me to a bird in a tree behind me, which I then listened to breathing.

By the time I arrived at the front of the house, Rosemary and Grace had barely made it to the bottom step. They were startled by my arrival, which surprised me since I knew they had seen me. "I thought I saw you across the yard," Grace said. I told her she had. "Did you run?" she asked. Did I run? No. On the contrary, time seemed to be moving very slowly indeed.

I stood for a moment in awkward conversation with the girls when I realized that as deafening as their heartbeats had been from across the lawn, at this proximity they were like booming percussion which I had trouble tuning out. I could still hear their words and their breathing, and at first what was annoying and overpowering eventually turned into a wondrous melody of life as I allowed the sounds to wash over me, not fighting them.

Not really having much to say to the girls, and knowing that they had plans, I quickly took my leave of them and resumed my way to the kitchen. Unintentionally I startled the cook. She accused me of sneaking up on her, though I was making no effort to keep my movements stealthy.

The aromas of the kitchen were miraculous! I could hardly wait to taste something – anything! I grabbed the nearest thing, a tomato from the table, and bit in. To my shock, never have I tasted something so foul! I could taste the cook's fingerprints on the flesh of the fruit. I could taste the residue from a snail which had crawled across the tomato surface only moments before it was plucked from the vine. I could taste which seeds were ripe, craving to be planted, and which ones were on the verge of rotting and already beginning to have the faintest rancid flavour. I grabbed something else – a crumb of bread. Yet the result was the same. I could taste the flour weevil eggs which had been hidden in the grains and milled with the flour and cooked into the bread. I could taste that a bit of eggshell had been left in one egg, and not properly washed, adding a hint of the flavour of the inside of a living chicken to the bread. I could taste that the cook had not cleaned her fingernails prior to kneading the dough and so had transferred remnants of her day's travels into it.

Food after food, the result was the same. Bite after bite I had to spit the food out, unable to tolerate all of the things I could taste, which otherwise I would not have been aware. The cook looked at me like I was crazy! And crazy I must have seemed, taking a bite of this and a bite of that, not being able to find anything to satisfy me.

I wonder why odours did not affect me thus. I could smell the rats hiding in the walls, covered in their own faecal matter. Cook herself was a veritable cornucopia of human odours. And yet even these unpleasant odours struck me as more interesting than disgusting. It was only the foods which I found intolerable. I left the kitchen.

Back out in the sun I had a moment of panic. What if the effects of this drug never wore off? I would never be able to eat again, and as such, I should starve to death in a matter of weeks. Could I even drink water or would I likewise be overcome with disgust, unable to even consume that most vital liquid?

Without a thought, I had begun to run. I didn't realize it until I was far away from the house. Deep in thought, I ran a tremendous distance and found myself back at my burned lab in what seems like only a matter of seconds, although I know, rationally, it must have taken much longer. I stopped at the lab, distracted now from my other concerns, and looked at the charred remains. As I stood there, my mind trying to make logic of what I was experiencing, I realized that for the whole run there I was not in the slightest bit tired or winded. I felt as though I could run all the way to London and still have no need to stop. And I did not sweat from the exertion.

The sunlight reflected off of broken pieces of glass and caught my eye, drawing it toward the remains of the wire cage where the fire must have started. Those unfortunate rats who gave their lives for science, left in a window to die.

I reached down and picked up that piece of broken window and sliced open the skin on my thumb. Perhaps the feeling of being super human had made me feel invincible so that I did not take any precaution in reaching for the glass. My thumb started to bleed and I did what I always do when I get a small cut on my hand – I stuck my thumb in my mouth to stop the bleeding. I had forgotten all about how horrible everything tasted and performed this motion by rote. To my amazement, my own blood did not taste horrible. It was actually sweet, yet savoury, and warm and delicious.

Did all blood taste this way? I thought back on the women in Madam DuPont's and the price I paid for my stash of elixir and wondered if they weren't constantly suffering the effects of the drug as well, unable to eat anything for the horrid flavour of it. And yet, they sustained themselves on one thing. Luckily for me, this will not become a concern. As long as I can stave off hunger for the few hours it takes for the drug to work its way through my system, I'll be fine.

I stood there, feeling like a super human, able to run miles in a matter of seconds without feeling tired, able to hear and see things over incredible distances with amazing detail, perhaps there was more which I had yet to discover. How conflicted I felt! My original purpose in studying the elixir was to help Felicity, and perhaps others, find some pleasure which was missing in their lives. And yet now I was presented with other aspects which I had never imagined possible, which I wasn't sure I wanted to share with anyone.

Imagine how much my life could improve by taking this drug and not telling anyone. Overhearing the secrets of the rich and powerful and using them to my own advantage. Even as I thought of this, I questioned my own morality. Is this the person I wanted to be? Was blackmail the best I could do with these abilities? I let the thought fall out of my mind and returned my attention to what seemed like more pressing matters – exploring what other changes this drug had instilled in me. I can scarcely remember the next few hours. I frolicked. I ran. I listened. I saw.

As I write this, I consider whether I should retire for the night or not. I am not yet tired and the drug is still in my system. The sun set a few hours ago and yet I can see as clearly as if it was high in the sky. Should I go explore the nocturnal world or allow sleep to overtake me, knowing that with all probability when I awake tomorrow morning I will once again be myself. Hungry, but able to eat and back to just myself.

5 September 1854

Despite my resolve to retire at a reasonable hour last night, I simply was not able to fall asleep. I stayed in bed awake for hours, waiting for the drug to metabolize enough so that I could find some comfort in slumber, yet it did not happen. Eventually I decided it was better to be up and active, exploring the world, than staying in a bed doing nothing.

The world of night was remarkable. It was so quiet and calm compared to the daytime world I was used to. I ran with abandon to the main house and scaled the walls, listening to the sleeping family within. Yes, I scaled the walls! Physically it seemed like there were no limitations on what I could do. I sat on the roof and looked up at the sky full of stars, marvelling at how bright everything looked, and yet how it still had a distinct look of night. It was not simply that it looked as if it was day, it was as though I could just see more than ever before. There were no shadows too dark that I could not penetrate their depths.

I started off fearing that in solitude the night would seem eternal, yet the sunrise came soon enough and after watching that glorious event through my new eyes, I returned to my cottage to make a more normal, conspicuous entrée to the day.

Nearly twenty-four hours after ingesting the solitary drop of liquid, and the effect had not yet abated. And here, another day nearly done as I write this, I must record that it has still not lessened to any noticeable degree. Perhaps another sleepless night is in my future.

All I can surmise is that I am a victim of my own miscalculation. The distilled liquid, free from any water which burned off, and unaffected by its particulate companion, is much more potent than I ever imagined. Even just one drop was more than any human should ever be exposed to at one time. Whatever danger Madam DuPont was trying to protect her clients from – starvation, perhaps – by only allowing them to be exposed to controlled quantities, I am dangerously close to undoing. In future, I shall dilute that drop a hundred, nay a thousand times so no one else experience such long-lasting effects.

The hunger had not yet become unbearable, but I was concerned what state my health would be in when this drug wears off if I had not been able to drink anything for several days. I decided to boil some water to see if by doing so I might make it palatable enough to ensure my own survival.

I removed the kettle from the stove prior to reaching boiling and tasted the water. I could taste the metal from the kettle, and there was nothing which I would consider refreshing in the drink, but it was palatable, much to my relief. I may not be able to eat, but at least I would be able to drink and wait out the drug.

I had a meeting with Wilkinson late in the morning. I did my best to behave "normal" as we discussed some upcoming events. He is planning a large party in late September, with a possible trip to Paris shortly after. I mentioned my sister's condition and how I would very much enjoy paying a visit to Spain. He seemed amenable to the idea. I am not entirely sure if he wants to accompany me, adding it onto the Paris trip, or if he will permit me time off so that I can make the journey on my own.

In preparation for the party, Wilkinson anticipates his wife will send him to London several times to help with arrangements and purchase supplies. He will leave it to my own discretion if I wish to accompany him on those trips.

As I walked near the kitchen, I overheard the cook outside. I went to see what she was doing and stumbled upon her slaughtering a chicken for dinner. She had just decapitated it and was draining its blood into a bucket. The smell of the blood was intoxicating. I inquired about why she was collecting the blood. But, no. She intended to create a stock using the it. Once the chicken was drained, I carried the bucket into the kitchen for her while she remained in the yard to pluck the bird.

Once in the kitchen, alone, I did something I never would have imagined. I tasted the chicken's blood. Inspired by tasting my own blood the day before, the chicken's blood was remarkably tasty. Was this the key to staving off starvation while under the influence of this drug? I do not know if chicken blood contains the nutrients needed to sustain human life, but for now it was my only option. I had a few good swallows and cleaned myself, all the while keeping my ears peeled for the sounds of anyone approaching. I could hear the cook outside expertly cleaning the bird. I could hear Wilkinson tapping his fingers on his desk on the other side of the house. I could hear Grace, still up in her bedroom, fretting over what to wear that day. It was impossible for me to be taken by surprise! I left the bucket on the table, the lower level of blood only perceptible to myself, and left the kitchen.

I spent most of the day sitting in the garden. To any passersby it probably seemed as if I was deep in thought. In truth, I was listening. Even though the house was several hundred yards away, I could hear all conversations within. I let my senses drift from room to room. It took a great deal of self-control to not linger long on Grace's private discussions with her sister. How easily I could see myself becoming corrupted by this ability and using it to my own advantage. How many more days before I would no longer be able to let those conversations rest, allowing my own curiosity to win out, listening to every private utterance?

I wondered if with a stronger dose perhaps I would not only hear conversations over such a distance, but if it was possible to hear thoughts. I could hear the blood circulating within the confines of skin and bone, is thought so much more distant that there is no amount of listening which can penetrate its secrets?

6 September 1854

I was not able to sleep last night, but circumstances were such that it did not matter. Shortly after I retired to my cottage, Wilkinson came to my door with a frantic neighbour, Mr. Youngblood. One of Youngblood's cows was having a difficulty. His farmhand was nowhere to be found. He remembered that Wilkinson had hired a private physician and thought perhaps I would be able to help.

Youngblood's property was several miles away so I packed a small bag, ready to stay there for the night, and we set off. I kept thinking to myself that it would have been so much faster for me to run to his property than taking the carriage, yet there was no logical way for me to excuse myself from the men's company and set off on foot. By the time we arrived at Youngblood's, the sun had set making it quite dark outside. Wilkinson and Youngblood went to the house to deposit our bags and to find some candles or torches. They pointed me in the direction of the stable.

Once their backs were turned, I set off in a flash for the stable and found the distressed cow in mere seconds. I could hear two heartbeats. I set about my work very quickly and was amazed at how my enhanced senses made my facility with the beast so quick. My hands were agile, certain in what to do, where to press, where to pull, to ensure that the calf would survive the ordeal.

I pulled the calf from inside its mother and stood there holding it. Yes! I stood there holding the full weight of the newborn calf. In the course of my normal day I had not need to lift something as heavy as a calf, and had someone told me I would be able to stand there holding one feeling it weigh on me no more than a newborn kitten would, I would have thought them insane. I heard Wilkinson and Youngblood approach and gently set the calf on the ground, returning to my work. I cleared the calf's nostrils and massaged its face and neck until it began breathing. Once the calf appeared to be stable, I returned my attention to the cow. She was tired, but her heartbeat was strangely steady. Because of how I was able to manipulate her calf and assist with the birth, I felt confident both of them would survive this night.

As the mother cow licked her baby clean, Wilkinson and Youngblood entered the stable with their candles and looked at me with astonishment. The stable was so dark they were amazed that I had located the pregnant cow, let alone helped her complete a successful birth already. And for a fleeting moment I felt smug and superior, taking credit for everything myself. Me. I had done this. I could do anything!

How easy it could be to get used to this... What a dangerous thing to consider.

Youngblood was hospitable, putting us up in two of his finest rooms for the night. Yet once again, I could not sleep. I lie in bed, listening to the sounds of Youngblood's house for the whole night. Just the sounds of a sleeping house and my own thoughts. And the thought which kept returning: What if this drug never wears off?

9 September 1854

The fear that the drug would never wear off was unfounded.

Those sleepless nights, time which the drug freely gave, and it took back from me as it vacated my system.

The return journey from Youngblood's farm was uneventful, but throughout the day I could feel the effects of the drug slipping away. I tried to listen to the music of life all around me, but could only hear my own breathing. I tried to see the vibrancy of life energy flowing through all things, yet I could see nothing more than I could a few days prior. By the time evening came, I was overcome with exhaustion and retired early. I cannot say with any certainty if I was awake long enough for the sun to set or if I won the race with the day to see which of us would retire first.

Much of what I report now is what has been told to me. The next morning, I failed to awaken and Wilkinson came to my cottage personally to see if I was in some kind of distress. He tried to get me out of bed and up to the house for breakfast, but I drifted in and out of consciousness and could not be moved. He became concerned that perhaps I had contracted some sort of illness on our brief journey to Youngblood's, and was worried that he also might have been afflicted. I was feverish and delirious.

Wilkinson, not wishing to expose anyone else in the house to a toxin or virus, brought food to me and checked on my status throughout the day. This careful watch he kept over me for the more than 24 hours.

After over a day of nearly uninterrupted sleep, I began to come to. I was still exhausted, unable to leave my cottage, still cared for by Wilkinson, but my memory began to return during this time. And I was even more acutely aware that I was, once again, normal. I think I even said this aloud at one point when Wilkinson was in the room. "Normal." He could not have known what I was talking about, but he assumed it was something to do with my illness and began to talk to me.

As my strength, my normal strength, returned, I assured Wilkinson that I was not contagious and that no one else in the house need be concerned about my illness. I could not explain to him what was wrong with me, at least not truthfully, so I told him I was sure I had contracted something in the stable. There was no need for worry. I also assured him that it was unlikely that the cow or newborn calf would be in any danger as my symptoms seemed specific to illnesses which only humans can contract, not livestock.

Finally, today I was able to resume most of my normal activities. Because I took such an extreme dosage of this drug during my experiment, I plan on waiting longer than the requisite week before testing the effects of the salt on myself. As an extra precaution, I will take a minute amount of it only. If it is not a large enough sample to experience any effect, I will try a larger dose in the following week.

Now that I am back to being myself, I feel a tremendous sense of loss. As difficult as it was for me to resist the euphoric effects of the elixir, it will be doubly as difficult to resist the distilled liquid drug. I already find my mind drifting to the subject of how to best dilute it for optimum effects with minimal risks. Is there a better delivery system? Should I have tried applying it to my skin rather than ingesting it directly? Inhaling it as steam? Will it dilute best in water or alcohol or some other liquid? If only I could try all approaches at once.

I fear my research is losing focus by my own personal interest. This substance is too dangerous to allow it to fall into the wrong hands and I still have no empirical data regarding the long-term exposure effects. Logically I know I should discontinue my experimentation. Waiting will be the biggest test of my willpower I have ever had to endure.

14 September 1854

Waiting for this day was nearly unbearable. When I was using rats for my experiments, I was not so overcome with temptation as I have been anticipating today when I taste the salt. My preparation is ready. I have studied the available grains and have found the smallest one. With a razor, I sliced it in half and in half again. This granule, smaller than a halite crystal, smaller than a grain of sand, is mine to savour.

I have mixed a preparation of my stimulating drug, as a precaution, and instructed Wilkinson that if he does not see me for two days he is to come to my cottage and administer the stimulant. I do not know if it will counteract the effects of the drug, but it is my only hope. Wilkinson pressed me to explain, but I did not. He finally agreed to do as I have asked. I pray that the dosage I have prepared is small enough that I will only be disabled for one night, or a portion thereof, but I must prepare for the worst. I underestimated the potency of the liquid, there is a chance that even with extra precautions I am underestimating the strength of the solid.

15 September 1854

The test was a success! I retired early and took the drug before the sun had set. Almost instantly I was overcome with the familiar feeling of bliss which I had come to know, and crave, since my first exposure to it in Japan. The one small crystal provided enough of the drug to last for approximately 15 hours, after which time I had a lingering sense of wellbeing which remained for several hours.

During the throws of the drug I was incapacitated. It was much more intense than what I could remember experiencing before. Every cell in my body tingled with pleasure. I longed for nothing. I didn't want to eat or walk or leave my cottage or move. I was sitting on the edge of my bed when I took the drug and when the sensation began to dissipate, I will still on the edge of my bed.

I remember the pleasure. One thing which I was concerned of was blacking out and remembering nothing of the experience, but I remember it all. And I didn't want it to end.

The lingering sensation was also wonderful. Never before have I felt so joyful and uplifted during the day for absolutely no reason. The world seemed like a more bright and cheerful place than I normally see. I noticed that the people I encountered seemed to have their moods improved for being around me. By being in a good mood, I was able to influence their moods.

This is the effect which I wish to focus on recreating. If I dilute the salt, take an even smaller quantity, perhaps I can reduce the time of the initial immobilizing bliss and extend the lingering sense of goodwill. How different would Felicity's life be if she could experience this joy for a day?

I must now wait another week.

16 September 1854

With the date of his party soon approaching, Wilkinson has decided it is necessary to make a trip into London to make some last-minute arrangements and purchases. Since I have been distracted by my experiments, I have asked to accompany him. It will do me good to be away from this place. We leave in the morning and will be gone for two days.

I have been considering the ramifications of continuing to experiment upon my own person and I have nearly convinced myself that it will not be dangerous. Aside from those rats which died in the fire, I witnessed no detrimental effects. If I decrease the dose of the salt so that I am only taking a proportional fraction of what I ingested day before last and dilute it, though I might take it several days in a row the overall quantity of the drug will be equivalent to the same dose I might otherwise take in one night. Surely there is no harm in this? I assume the harm comes from quantity and not duration of exposure, although since I don't know what the harm is, I could be incorrect.

I have decided to use an atomizer to administer the drug in my next round of experiments rather than ingesting the preparation directly. This will further dilute the administered dose, at the same time mimicking the method of delivery Madam DuPont employs.

I must try and push it out of my head now for a few days. And what better distraction than the party! I have learned only a few details of the event, but the most important of these is that the party is for Grace. In London I must make the most of my time. I'll be fitted for a new suit. I will also see if I cannot find some small token gift for Grace, although I am not certain if gifts are appropriate for the event. Perhaps I will be able to squeeze some information from Wilkinson during the train ride – what better time to loosen a man's tongue than when confined in a compartment for hours. There will be nothing for us to do other than talk or stare out the window, and it is a view he has seen countless times.

There will be dancing at the party. I must write to Isabel to thank her for insisting that I be her partner in learning to dance. I will be able to dazzle Grace with my dancing and she shall see that it was erroneous to consider me "old."

What pleasant dreams I expect to have this evening, dancing with Grace all through the night.

18 September 1854

Wilkinson had many things to attend to during the day and we set off on independent courses. He did not know how long his tasks would take so he freed me from any obligation of meeting back with him at the flat to dine. My day in London was all mine.

I set off first thing for the tailor's so that I could purchase a new suit and have it fitted. I hoped that with enough financial incentive they might even be able to perform the alterations the very same day. The tailor had a daughter. She must have been around nineteen. Pretty as could be. Any man would have been crazy to not find her attractive. I found her attractive.

As I was spending the day alone, and needed to find a gift for Grace (Wilkinson said it would not be inappropriate to present her with a small gift at the affair if I felt so moved), I decided to ask this girl, Sophia, if she had any suggests of where I might go or what I might buy. With little persuading, Sophia decided it would be best if she spent the day with me, convinced I would not buy an appropriate gift if left to my own devices. I have no doubt that she also believed there might be a duplicate gift purchased for her if she showed proper enthusiasm, as well as a meal or two for spending the day with me. She was correct on both accounts.

Ironically, she took me to an all too familiar location – back to my own old office to visit Eugene, the perfumer, and select one of those delicate bottles of perfume. Eugene remembered me from our last visit and was pleased to see me. I allowed Sophia to select something and made a gift of it for her. One of the bottles I already had at home would be the perfect gift for Grace.

We returned to the tailor's near five and the suit was ready. He was able to work on it that day and had few interruptions. I tried it on and was satisfied with the fit. I invited Sophia out to dinner.

It was such a pleasant diversion to spend the day with a beautiful young woman that I hardly thought of my work at all. By the time I returned to the house, Wilkinson was still not home. So here I am, alone. Just me and my thoughts. A most dangerous combination.

19 September 1854

Barely back in the country and already my mind returns to my work.

I have a bad habit, which I learned long ago to avoid -- beginning new work late in the day. Although it is rare that I am as consumed by my work as I currently am, it is not rare that I will become so interested in the process of study that I forget the mundane details of life. How many nights have I spent hovering over test tubes? Pouring over stacks of papers? Dissecting beasts of all sizes? And to what end? Only one: knowledge. Lost sleep. Unbearable hunger pangs. Thirst so powerful that my body refused to continue doing my bidding until I provided it with that vital fluid water.

No, if I begin something now, I know that my own curiosity will propel me to a sleepless night, which is something I have experienced far too frequently of late.

Last night, in London, I found that my sleep was not as sound as I would have hoped. While I was not fully awake the whole night, deep, restful sleep eluded me. My mind was racing with so many thoughts. I have no doubt this was the cause of my temporary restless state. Will Grace like her gift? Will my experiments yield the desired results quickly or am I only at the beginning of a laborious study? Will my supply of the elixir last long enough for me to reach any valid conclusions? Although I have done a fair amount of study of the properties of the elixir, I am no closer this evening than I was in Japan to knowing the components of the substance. Perhaps that should have been my original goal. Copy it first, then discover all of the secrets it holds. Yet the effects are what fascinate me and the ability to synthesize it seems trivial in comparison.

The supply will last. I feel confident that once diluted, the salt will be of a suitable strength to deliver the exact effect I desire. And at such a diluted proportion, the supply I have, although scarcely more than one teaspoon full, will last for months or even years. If I have not been able to synthesize the drug in that time, perhaps I will have procured an alternate source – a hope which I have not yet abandoned. The liquid, although of great personal interest, is not the substance to which I should devote my time.

The trip to London came at the perfect time. I shall resume my studies tomorrow, nearly one week after my last trial, and I feel confident that in the revised, smaller dose, I shall suffer no ill effects for continuing to experiment upon myself.

20 September 1854

My first experiment with the diluted and atomized salt was a success! I awake this morning as the sun was just peering over the horizon. That gave me time to myself before the household would really come to life. Only Cook and some house staff would be out and about this early.

I immediately set to work, adding my fractional grain of salt to one of the full bottles of perfume. The salt dissolved in a matter of seconds. I forced myself to wait several minutes, agitating the mixture to ensure the salt compound was evenly distributed in the fragrant alcohol.

If my calculations were off, I could remain catatonic for several hours before my absence would be noted. I sat comfortably on the foot of my bed and sprayed the perfume onto my wrist as I had seen Isabel do.

I could smell the aroma drift through the air, but felt no immediate effect. I wondered if I should add more salt to the mixture or if contact with my skin wasn't enough for the drug to take hold.

I brought my wrist to my nose and inhaled deeply. That was the key!

As soon as I smelled the perfume fully, I was seized by the immobilizing pleasure I sought. If it lasted even as long as a second, I cannot say. I sniffed my wrist again and again, each time being overcome by the feeling of bliss which rendered me helpless. But each time the feeling lasted only slightly past the duration of my deep inhalation. I must have spent an hour in this repetitive fashion before finally convincing myself to stop abusing the substance and to return to my objective.

I ventured outside and rubbed grass and mud on my wrist to wipe away the scent, lest I accidentally infect members of the household with it.

A great feeling of wellbeing and happiness stayed with me until around noon. Although without more study I won't know if the duration of this was caused by my frequent inhalations or just a byproduct of an advance in my research.

21 September 1854

I repeated the same experiment today, using the bottle of perfume I prepared yesterday. I have marked this particular bottle so I don't confuse it with the others.

I restrained myself and only permitted one deep inhalation of the perfume. The euphoria lasted just as briefly as yesterday. The lingering effects lasted for two hours. Not as long as yesterday when I overindulged in my whiffs. To make an effective potion for Rosemary, I'm considering adding more salt.

24 September 1854

My Dearest Isabel,

I found myself thinking of you all day and decided that the best way to ease my mind was to write to you. I know that I am several weeks premature in anticipating a return letter from you, but your wellbeing is a great concern to me. I will be traveling to Spain in approximately one month's time and hope to have some word of where you are staying prior to my voyage.

I must confess that I have been suffering from insomnia of late and thus have spent many long nights in only the shallowest of sleep, drifting in and out of consciousness. It is not that I am completely without sleep, but the sleep that I have is not restful and there are many hours during the night when I share the darkness with my own thoughts. Often those thoughts turn to you.

When I do manage to sleep, I am overcome with vivid dreams. When I awaken from them, I am clammy and shivering, my pulse racing.

Please write and tell me that you have had a successful birth and that I am an uncle! This would be celebratory enough that even I would spend time with our parents for the pleasure of seeing my niece or nephew. My fondest hope for my visit is to find you happy and nursing a healthy baby.

Perhaps the cause of my restlessness is nothing more than an overactive mind. I am consumed by my work, concerned about you, and excited about the impending ball I find myself dancing instead of walking, practicing so that I may ask Grace to dance and impress her with my agility, for which I have you to thank.

It is all interconnected. You, the dancing, the ball, my work, my insomnia. I am certain once one of these is resolved, the others will sort themselves out.

I hope that by the time I come visit I shall be able to share the secrets I am uncovering in my research. It is so exciting for me and I long to be able to share it with someone.

Please write soon. I'll keep you in my thoughts.

Love,

Diego

24 September 1854

I had the most vivid dream last night. I nearly wrote the dream to Isabel, but then remembered that I have not yet shared the results of my experiments with her and did not want to confuse her. I shall share my experiments with her soon, but the time is not yet right.

In the dream, I was here, in my cottage, suffering from insomnia as I have been for the past few nights. I then began to listen to the dark, night-time world, and realized that my senses were awakened as they had been when I drank the liquid elixir.

I suppose that some part of my mind was aware that I was dreaming, because I did not have the same moral objection to eavesdropping on Grace that I had before. I concentrated and listened and heard the sounds of the house. I could see the house in my mind as I imagined a mist traveling across the lawn toward the house. Through the mist I found Grace's room and listened for her to fall asleep.

What happened next is somewhat disjointed, as dreams often are. I remember standing at the base of the wall just beneath Grace's window. No memory of how I came to be there. Then before I even had time to consider where I was or what I was doing, I began to scale the wall. My fingertips were able to find purchase in the smallest of cracks and it seemed as if my body was so light that it took no strength to propel myself up the steep building. I travelled almost as if by will. To a spectator perhaps I resembled a spider, clinging to the building impossibly. Or perhaps it appeared more like I flew up the side, not touching the building at all.

Then again time seemed to skip. I was standing inside of Grace's room. The window was open, the curtains billowing in a gentle breeze, so I surmised that I entered the room through that open window. I listened to Grace's sleep. I watched her. Although the room was as black as pitch, I could see her as if she was bathed in light. I could not resist approaching the bed, standing so near to her that I could feel her breath upon my skin.

I once again wondered if I listened carefully enough, I might be able to hear her thoughts. I watched and I listened. Part of me hoped that she would wake up and find me there. I imaged how she would react. She would, I thought, cry out in fright. I would need to restrain her. We would struggle and I would easily overpower her. Then she would see me as powerful, in command – how she did not see me now.

But she did not wake up. She rolled over and I was the one who was startled. Time skipped and I found myself back out on the lawn. I listened to the night once again and heard Grace through the din. She had not awakened. But rather than return to watch her sleep on, I listened to the animals sleeping in their burrows and nests and realized I was hungry.

I felt a wildness overtake me, but then I awoke. Back in my bed. It was still dark outside. I listened to the night, but the only blood flow I could hear was my own as my pulse raced, riled up from the dream. The only breathing I heard was my own. I was alone and I was, as I had been all night, in my cottage.

Sleep did not return that night. I remained awake, pondering the same issues which have plagued me the past several days. If the dream revealed anything to me, I think it is that I will not be satisfied leaving the liquid drug alone. Even something as simple as listening to Grace sleep became a miraculous event in the dream – something which is not possible to recreate without continued study of the liquid.

29 September 1854

Is there a point in the pursuit of love that morality must be called into question? Night after night I have had the same dream of watching Grace while she sleeps. It varies little. And when I awaken, I wonder this: if the end result of any action is a happy long life with the woman I love, can the action itself be held in contempt? Isn't any means justified when the end result is as righteous as love?

I overheard Grace discussing the final party arrangements with her mother and learned that carnations are her favourite flower. This is information I have come by accidentally, but which nonetheless was not disclosed to me personally. If I were to use it to my advantage, present Grace with a bouquet of carnations, Grace might be inclined to believe that we both share of love of that flower. It would be one small link in the chain of endearing me to her. I would never disclose to her the truth – that while I do enjoy flowers, I do not have a favourite and that if I were forced to choose, it would not be something as common as a carnation. From the day I overheard this until the end of my life with Grace, the carnation will be, must be, my favourite flower.

Similarly, if the opportunity ever arose to learn more details of Grace's taste which I could exploit, shouldn't I take that opportunity? Could I – or anyone – resist the desire to read the diary of a loved one to learn their most secret feelings and desires? And in knowing you would not be caught doing so, wouldn't that same reasonable person treat those secrets as gold? Spending them at the most opportune time to gain the object they desired, love?

Spending time together and being alert, these same secrets could probably be learned through somewhat less devious means. If Grace and I were to stroll together through the garden, I could say something like, "Don't you just adore roses?" and her reply would be, "They are lovely, but carnations are far more beautiful." Then it is a matter of being thoughtful and remembering those small moments and conversations. The connection would not be the same, though. Grace would somehow remember, even if subconsciously, that I did not share her love of carnations. Instead I would be praised for my good memory and attention. A stronger bond is created by sharing a similarity, not be being thoughtful.

I am so confused! Perhaps I am trying to justify some behaviour to which I have yet to succumb. If I reconcile the act within myself prior to committing it, I expect to feel no guilt after. But what, exactly, am I planning? Even this is not clear to me. It was by chance that I learned Grace's favourite flower. I cannot rely on chance to provide me with more such opportunities. Do I intend to linger in dark corners, hoping for Grace and her mother or sister to pass? And should I be fortunate enough that they do, do I honestly expect that their discussions will yield fruit?

How frustrating that this consumes my thoughts. I have so much work to attend to, and yet I lose whole hours contemplating how to infiltrate Grace's world. Trickery. Deception. Lies. Secrets. These are my weapons in a battle only I know exists. Grace is the prize. Is any weapon to be overlooked?

1 October 1854

I am writing in the wee hours of the morning, rather than on my usual schedule, so that my memory might be preserved as accurately as possible. Grace's party is still going on, although winding down significantly enough that I felt it was acceptable for me to take my leave.

All day yesterday Wilkinson had friends and family arriving from all over England, and now they are all staying the night, some a few days longer, in that huge mansion he shares with his small family and servants. If it were possible for a house to be happy, I would say that the house was the happiest it has been all summer to have each room filled with conversation and laughter. And, although I am not antisocial by nature, I have found great comfort in being able to retire to the privacy of my own little cottage rather than also spending the night in that overflowing house.

But the night was not the joyous occasion for which I had hoped. I had assumed that we were celebrating Grace's birthday, or perhaps some other anniversary or occasion, so my heart sank when Wilkinson clinked the champagne glasses to silence the room so that he could announce the engagement of Grace and David. But I get ahead of myself.

Wilkinson prevailed upon my services as a spare pair of hands early in the day so that I might help carry in crates of supplies which were still arriving that morning. I diligently assisted and was not able to return to my cottage to clean and dress until the party was just about to begin, causing my late arrival.

While in my cottage, I know not what possessed me to do this, but I took a small phial, one which holds only ten millilitres of liquid, and filled it with water. I then took a pin and dipped the very tip in my liquid extract, swirling the pin through the water. I sealed the phial and carried it in my pocket to the party. The extract was diluted, far less than the drop I had taken before, but the quantity was untested. Thinking back on it now I see how foolish it was. But at the time, I thought only of gaining advantage in my pursuit of Grace, through any means.

Once I was dressed (which I did with haste), I found the perfume bottle intended to present to Grace and left my cottage for the night. I feared for a moment that I had picked up the wrong bottle – I have been using one bottle of the perfume as a medium for the dissolved salt – but I found my marked bottle and satisfied myself that I had taken the intended one. (I shall have to write a more detailed report of my studies with it at some future date.)

I suppose it was fortunate that I did arrive at the party late. It prevented some awkward conversation while waiting for the room to fill up. A late arrival at a busy party is far less conspicuous than the early arrival when the room is empty. I made the rounds, talking to Wilkinson's business associates whom I had met in passing in London, visiting with family members, and being something of a local town hero for delivering Youngblood's cow at great personal risk – that story had grown into something of a folk tale! I'll have to pass that story along to Isabel to add to her collection of stories to tell her son, about the doctor who delivered a calf in the pitch blackness in a disease-infested stable only to come down with a life-threatening disease which he could not cure himself of, but which he somehow managed to recover from. If only they knew the real story, which is just as fantastic!

It was a welcome change to talk about something even remotely related to medicine instead of the usual conversation I had here in London – how I was a foreigner. What did I think of the country? My, my English was good. When would I find a good Spanish senorita and settle down? I felt like I had passed some initiation and that these people thought of me as one of their own. Willing to risk his life for their livelihood.

Some of Wilkinson's business associates also asked about our trip to the Far East. I was able to tell the story of bringing back a fertility idol for two of my patients, and, with a wink, how I hoped to check on the results soon. I was able to also discuss, with no detail, some of my current research and what I hoped to discover. I didn't reveal any of my true secrets, but I did share how I was hoping to find a substance which could enhance a person's mood. We discussed the inspiration for all of my studies – my patients – and the more savvy among them wondered how I would continue to find inspiration working for only one client now. I assured them that there were things in the country to inspire a man.

I politely conversed with David for a time as well. He had the same questions, wanting to hear about the Youngblood event. I reminded myself to not hold it against the man that he and Grace were so familiar, and to try and judge him instead on his own merits, but it was a challenge. As soon as I was able to excuse myself from his company, I did.

As late as I was arriving at the party, Wilkinson's daughters were even later. Rosemary was first to arrive. She looked lovely. I shouldn't be surprised if taken off and measured the diameter of her skirt at the bottom it wouldn't turn out to be taller than the girl! It was so full and ruffled. I admired how well she managed it, not tripping once that I saw. She shared her first dance with Robert, and I invited the daughter of one of Wilkinson's associates to dance.

Her name was Jasmine. She was small. Delicate. An excellent dancer. It was a pleasure to dance with her, yet again I had that feeling that I was betraying Grace by even taking the liberty of enjoying myself in the innocent company of another woman.

There is something in Grace, and to some degree in all women, of the exhibitionist. Wanting to be the centre of attention. Grace's delayed arrival at the party was clearly orchestrated to appease her desire to be seen. She did not make an appearance until all of the guests had arrived. She came in through a terrace door, the wind blowing her hair and causing her scarf to billow. No one in the room could ignore the breeze as it wafted through, and all turned their heads to see what the cause was.

Her dress was not full like her little sisters. Long and slim to her body, covered with silken flowers, rosettes and ribbons. The dress itself a work of art, full of life, movement and vibrancy. She was life.

She glided across the room and kissed her father on the cheek, and then she took David's hand.

That was when Wilkinson clinked on his champagne glass. The longer he talked, the less I could hear. My face flushed and I could only hear the pounding of my own heart. Before he finished his speech, feeling faint, I left the party. But my absence was to be short-lived and to go unnoticed.

Outside, with the cool evening air blowing against my skin, quickly drying the perspiration which had begun to form on my brown, I remembered the phial in my pocket and I assumed that it was the hand of fate which had moved me earlier that day to place it there. And who was I to ignore the hand of fate? Although they were engaged, they were not yet married. It only meant that I needed to become more serious in my pursuit and use every weapon available to sway Grace's favour away from David and toward me. As a normal man, I hadn't had any luck so far, but as a superman, perhaps I would be harder to resist.

I drank the entire contents of the phial and I immediately began to pray that the diluted quantity would be enough to affect a change in me. I decided to return to the party and not stand outside waiting for the drug to work. From my previous experience with it, it wasn't something which presented any signals once it was working, it just would work. It was up to me to be aware of it, and I had no doubt I would be aware.

I did take a moment to calm myself down, put on a façade of joy for the young couple, and returned to the party.

Back inside, the dancing has resumed. Grace and David danced together and although I did not want to be conspicuous, I stared at them openly. At least, under the circumstances, I was not alone in my gawking. Many eyes were on the pair, it was their night. Their party. I felt someone tapping me on the shoulder and turned to see young Rosemary. I was broken from my trance.

I asked Rosemary to dance and out we went onto the dance floor. As we twirled, I suddenly realized that the drug was working. Although they were also dancing, coming and going, covering the entire area of the ballroom, I had been listening to their conversation out of all of the concurrent conversations taking place. Not wanting to neglect Rosemary, and hoping to gain some favour with her sister by being tolerant and charming with the child, I returned my attention to Rosemary and took the opportunity to show everyone in the room how skilled a dancer I was.

 Then came one of the cruellest reminders of them all. Once the dance ended, Wilkinson came over and told Rosemary that it was time for her to leave the party and go to sleep. He then asked me, as one of his employees, to see Rosemary to her room. While I do understand that Wilkinson is my employer, I find it difficult at times to hold my tongue and do his bidding. I bore Rosemary no ill will, and would have been content to escort her to her room on any other occasion, but on this night I wanted to not only remain present at the party, I also wanted to make a good impression on Grace – something I could scarcely do if I were absent. My only hope was that Grace would notice that I was being kind to her sister and that this would gain me some small favour.

Rosemary was pleased that I was chosen to see her to her room that evening. I knew that I was the object of her schoolgirl crush, a secret I wish I did not know and which if she ever found out I knew would horrify her. She did her best to flirt with me in a clumsy, immature way as we walked through the dark, empty house, the sounds of the party fading into the background. And I did my best to humour her without giving encouragement. I also tried to conceal my impatience as she seemed determined to make the walk into something of a leisurely romantic stroll.

How long did I have until the drug wore off? Unknown. And was this to be how I spent the night? Tucking a child into bed? As soon as we reached her room, I gently escorted her inside and shut the door. I could hear her reopen the door and call for me, but I took off running as swiftly as I could and before her hand had even come away from the handle, I was halfway to my cottage.

The only other weapon in my arsenal was the salt, and although I did not want to expose Grace to the entire contents of the bottle by presenting that perfume bottle to her, I did want her to experience the euphoria of it, and with my heightened reflexes I decided that I should try a little sleight of hand.

I returned to the party through the same door by which I had left and finally, feeling perhaps overly confident, I approached Grace. I presented her with the original perfume bottle and was disappointed by her reaction. She barely took a sniff before setting it on a table. She was polite, as her breeding had taught her to be, but her dismissive response to the gift made her true feelings clear. I picked the bottle back up and insisted that she should try some on – that I had the scent specifically blended in London and that I thought she would be rather impressed by it once it was freed from its glass confinement. I took her hand, kissed the back, then turned her wrist skyward. With movements so quick that no human would have seen them, I then sprayed on spritz of the salted perfume on her delicate flesh and quickly returned the laced bottle to my pocket and the gift bottle to the table. I was still in control of her hand as I gently bent her arm and brought her wrist up close to her face so that she could smell the aroma.

As I anticipated, she was hit with a sudden rush of ecstasy. I pulled her close, pushed her head beside mine and whispered in her ear, "I hope you have found the happiness you deserve." The ecstasy was fleeting, as I had designed, and as I sensed her pulse slow, I released my grip on her and kissed her hand. I asked her to dance, and although she did not know the reason, she was unable to resist.

I could tell by her expression that she had settled into the general lingering contentment the salt creates, and as the music I asked her if she would now give me her considered opinion of the perfume. "My favourite," she said. "I'm glad you reconsidered," I answered. "You should always be willing to reconsider." And with that, I made for the exit.

How delicate the fabric of a relationship is. I wanted nothing more than to remain at the party, to tell Grace exactly how I feel about her, but I must treat her like a wild animal being stalked in the woods. If I make a wrong move, rustle the leaves under my feet too loudly, she could become too frightened for any progress to ever be made. So now I must wait and hope that my efforts this evening were sufficient to plant a seed of doubt in her mind that perhaps David is not the only man suited for her, that perhaps there is another, better option.

On my way out, I encountered David. I offered him my congratulations and shook his hand, but as he stood there, smiling, being gracious, I began to feel a burning in my chest. Jealousy and rage the likes of which I have never felt before began to bubble to the surface. Who was this man and why did fortune decide to smile on him? There was nothing extraordinary about him. Fair hair, thin build, moderate height. I had not had occasion to have any conversation with him, but nothing in his countenance suggested that he was of remarkable intellect. Average, average, average.

My emotion ran – dare I even write the word? —toward murderous. I decided that it was better to appear rude than to allow this encounter to continue and possibly to become dangerous (to his life and my cause), and did not even bother making an excuse as I left him standing there, mid-sentence.

I have been sitting alone in my cottage for an hour or more now, listening to the party. The guests have finally begun to retire and Wilkinson has confided in his wife that he hopes the remaining guests tire soon or he will be forced to leave the party before they do, something which he does not regard as proper host behaviour. Grace has been polite in her acceptance of good cheer from the guests, but she has lost some of her enthusiasm for the event. I hope it is not only from her fatigue, but that she has been influenced by my spell.

1 October 1854 (later)

I cannot say for certain what time the drug wore off, but the last thing I remember, lying in bed listening to the party, was hearing Grace ask someone, "Did Diego leave?" "Did Diego leave"! Three small words, but how I have longed to even have her speak my name! And as quickly as my plan was set in motion, I must once again abandon it and return to my job of being at Wilkinson's beck and call.

I write this entry from London. Yes, back in London. Wilkinson came to my door very early in the morning and awakened me, instructing that I should pack up the entire contents of my cottage and one traveling bag. We left before noon, many of the party guests still lingering at the house, others having already scattered to the wind, and began yet another of his business trips. While we are gone, Lady Wilkinson will pack up the main house and the family will leave the house in the country and return to London now that summer was quite over and the weather has begun to turn cool.

On the train ride, he explained that after years of experience, he found it was best to not be in his wife's way when it was time to pack up and move the house. He never packed the right things and she would end up yelling at him. Although she resented him the first year he left her to pack up on her own, she soon came around to his way of thinking and decided that it was better for them both that he leave during the move, having nothing useful to contribute.

We were to stay in London for a couple of days while Wilkinson made arrangements from that end for the family's return. The house was stuffy and dusty from disuse. When we stayed there, we had no servants, using it as little more than a ready hotel. A room with a bed. Wilkinson would need to hire some people to help him air it out and clean the linens, freshen the place. And then we would head south. Until the arrangements were all settled, I was free to do what I wanted in London.

It was frustrating that he insisted I come with him and not come up a few days later, once he had some of the arrangements sorted. I have finally made some progress with Grace, and here I didn't even get to say goodbye to her before being whisked away. How long will this journey be? Undetermined. "Did Diego leave?" Yes, Grace. I've gone. I only hope that I have planted enough doubt in your mind that when I see you again, the old cliché will ring true – that absence had made the heart grow fonder.

24 September 1854

Dear Doctor Amador,

I was surprised to receive your letter. I must admit that I believed there was some trickery on your part when last we saw one another, and that you were not truly immune to our influence as you claimed. Yet the fact that you have not yet uncovered all of the secrets of this fluid, have not learned to "synthesize" it on your own, as you put it, makes me reconsider that opinion. Either you are immune, or you are a man of remarkable restraint. Which is it? Don't answer, it isn't important.

I've enclosed for you a little gift. Two gifts, actually. First, yes, I have a sister and it would give me great pleasure if you were to torment her. How callous of me to admit, yet there it is.

I cannot tell you how many years she made my life a living hell in Paris, and to make you a thorn in her side would not even begin to repay her, but I'll consider it a start.

The second gift is a sample to tide you over (assuming your supply has run dry) until you are able to locate and strike a bargain with my sister. If you have been partaking yourself, and not keeping the samples for your "research," then I highly recommend that you not share this one. Consider it a rare vintage.

If you do find my sister, please do the kindness of letting me know – providing me complete details of how you blackmail her and how much she squirms under your influence. It will be hollow for me to have no report.

Do not ask me for additional information. As you can surmise, I have not kept up with my sister's life. This is the only information I have on her. Perhaps it is out of date, perhaps you will find her with ease. Either way, it is in the hands of fate now.

Bonne continuation,

Madame Géneviève DuPont

2 October 1854

I retrieved a letter from Madam DuPont today. Enclosed with it she included a small cobalt bottle, sealed with wax. I have not opened it yet, but based on her letter, I deduce that it contains my elixir.

The bottle answers one question I did have – assuming that Madam DuPont has more intimate knowledge of it that I do, which I must – which was the extent of the photo-reactive properties on the elixir. She felt that cobalt glass was opaque enough to prevent an explosion should the bottle have somehow become exposed to light during the journey, and since it has arrived here safely, it must have been. Although the brothel had the windows blackened and curtains drawn, stained glass may have been just as effective at preventing disaster, although it would have allowed for prying eyes.

Ah! Each answer brings with it additional questions and avenues of study. I wonder if I shall ever feel I have exhausted my research of this liquid.

Madam DuPont was able to provide a name and address for her sister, although she admits the address is old and may not be accurate. At least with a name, I have somewhere to start.

That was the main excitement of my day today, retrieving my letter, which turned out to be a small parcel. I had provided Madam DuPont with my old address, hoping that Eugene would remember me well enough to hold the letter until I returned to London to retrieve it. I did not tell him I was expecting a letter, lest someone come in person and question him. The less he knows, the better off he'll be.

He was pleased to see me and had kept the parcel hoping that I would stop by when I was next in London. He remembered that I had mentioned having my office in the same location as his shop, so it was easy for him to assume that an acquaintance in Japan had not been informed of my new address yet. For my part, I was able to tell him that Grace had a strong response to his perfume. He was pleased to hear a review of his work.

After a short visit with Eugene, I returned to the house, eager to read my letter and learn what was in the box. I spent the rest of the afternoon staring at that small, cobalt bottle, weighing my options. It is at this moment unopened in my medical bag, carefully wrapped in cloth to prevent it from clinking on something and breaking.

3 October 1854

I tried to see Felicity today, but she refused to open the door to me. It is such a struggle to hold back on my discoveries, to keep them to myself, until I am sure that I fully understand them and can be certain that I am not ultimately doing more harm than good by exposing others to them. Even now I am conflicted over how I behaved during the party with Grace. So much so that I could not yet present the modified elixir to Felicity even though I know that the smallest exposure to it would transform her into a new, happier person.

Perhaps, though, it is not my place to even question these things. When I made the decision to become a doctor, it was at that same instant that I made the decision to disassociate myself from others to the degree where I could look upon them as machines needing repair. As a machine, Felicity is in need of repair. But I cannot undertake those repairs until I am reasonably certain that my actions will truly help. Small setbacks, accidents or bad reactions to treatment – these are to be expected. But to knowingly use a drug on someone when the drug is itself new and relatively untested borders on the reckless.

I thought of filling a perfume atomizer with only enough for one spray so that her exposure would be guaranteed to be limited to one treatment only. I thought of dousing a rose with the spray and leaving it on her doorstep, hoping that fate would intervene and induce her to sniff the flower and be exposed that way. Ultimately, until I can regain some of her trust, I dare not expose her to the drug. One treatment only and then my running off to France and Spain could be more detrimental than her current frame of mind. Once she has felt the joy, will her normal tormented state be even more unbearable for her?

Felicity shouted at me through the door to go away, only not in such nice terms. I did not let this deter me as I had on a previous visit. I remained outside, carrying on one half of a civil conversation with the door, ignoring the shouts and obscenities. I was there for a very long time considering I was talking to myself. I only hope that she listened to at least some of what I said so that the next time I am in London she might have softened some and will considered opening the door to me, or at least not shouting over me.

One thing which distracted me all day was that for some reason Grace was on my mind more than usual. I do not know why this should have been, but things kept reminding me of her. A breeze would rustle through the leaves, and out of nowhere, I would be reminded of Grace. I would turn my head at a certain angle, and think of Grace. There was no provocation. I was not visiting places where I had memories of Grace. I only mention this because it was so unusual. Me thinking of Grace in itself is not unusual. It is not something which would only happen at certain times. I am prone to have thoughts of Grace hovering just beneath the surface of my conscious thought at all times, but there was something so immediate and vital about these thoughts. At moments I would turn a full circle, just to make sure she wasn't somehow walking behind me.

4 October 1854

Now comes the question – is it merely coincidence, or has something truly otherworldly occurred? I went to visit Mary and Thomas today, just stopped by in the morning for a quick hello, and learned that after what seems like a lifetime of trying, all signs indicate that Mary is pregnant. It is still early days, but they are optimistic that it is not a fluke or illness presenting itself in a similar fashion and that in eight months' time they will have the child they have dreamed of for so long.

It was scarcely a month ago that I last saw them, bringing them the fertility idol I had found on my journey east. Short of taking the idol and placing it in the homes of married couples and seeing if they conceive, which lacks all scientific credibility, there is no way to prove or disprove the idol's effectiveness. I suppose it will make a good story in my dotage, if nothing more.

After a pleasant visit with them, I returned to the house to meet up with Wilkinson. He had made arrangements to visit a colleague after lunch, a man who specialized also in importing rare commodities.

While cleaning up for lunch, I noticed a stray hair on the coat I had worn the day before – one of Grace's. As absurd as it seems, I wonder if that was why she was on my mind so strongly yesterday. I was wearing a small part of her, and although I had though the drug had completely worn off, it could have left some residual, lingering effects. I must have looked like a madman after finding the hair and having this idea – I made circles around the room, sniffing the air. Alas, I could smell nothing more potent than the stale odour of air which had spent a summer uncirculated in a lifeless mansion.

Wilkinson and I ate together and went to visit with his friend, Dominic Stephens. Mr Stephens showed us to a shed in his yard where his latest acquisition was held – an albino python. We arrived just in time to watch the beast feed, an event which we were assured we were lucky to be witnessing because it happened rarely. Stephens took a large, healthy rabbit out of a hutch in the yard on the way to the shed, and although it appeared that he was holding the rabbit lovingly in his arms, once we entered the shed, Stephens took the defenceless creature by the feet and slammed its head against a concrete block, killing it in one violent blow. I didn't know how to react and watched in horror.

The rabbit's body limp, Stephens opened the python's cage and dangled the prize in front of the snake. The snake's eyes were expressionless. What was this creature thinking, seeing its next meal? Excitement? Anticipation? Hunger? Pity?

Stephens dropped the rabbit in front of the snake and closed the cage door. The monstrous phantom sprang at its prey, encircling it with powerful coils. Its body was one muscle which worked with deadly precision. Satisfied the rabbit was dead and ready to eat, the snake opened its mouth wider that appeared possible, and began to swallow the rabbit whole.

I did not want to appear squeamish and kept an unbreaking gaze on the spectacle. I tried to focus on the scientific aspects of what I witnessed. Comparing this snake to the cobras I had seen in Africa.

Mr Stephens was kind enough to provide commentary to the gruesome event, giving Wilkinson and I a rudimentary understanding of the snake's physiology. Without venom, the python constricts its prey, squeezing the life out of any creature it is able to overtake. The actual cause of death is asphyxiation. Under the pressure of the coils the prey cannot continue to breath. This snake was small in comparison to how large they could grow. At their worst, they were rumoured to be fierce man-eaters, with a particular appetite for human children.

I have no doubt that Mr Stephens was given to hyperbole, but it would not surprise me that a snake, if large enough, would give no second thought of making a meal of a man. A man certainly would not give a second thought of making a meal of a snake, under the right circumstances.

He had acquired this specimen on a recent journey to Borneo. I did not ask what the fate of the poor, caged creature might be. I suspected that in the end, the snake might suffer a similar fate as the rabbit. Or perhaps he intended to raise the snake to a mammoth size and test the theory of it being a man-eater. I was relieved we were there as friends of this man, and not enemies he wished to dispose of quietly and mysteriously in the night. The belly of a well-fed snake is no place to end one's life.

After watching the snake fressen, we returned to more congenial surroundings and enjoyed an aperitif. I was permitted to peruse the library while Wilkinson and his old chum reminisced. The library was filled with volume after volume on animal biology. Every creature known to man was catalogued in this place, with notes added by Stephens himself where he found discrepancies with the original text. I inquired as to his curiosity with wildlife and his only answer was that it was a hobby. Something which made his actual job more interesting. More bearable.

As the night grew long, Wilkinson invited Stephens to go out and dine with us, which he did. On our walk home, Wilkinson filled in some missing details on Mr Stephens profession. He was an exotic animal smuggler. Any animal with a price on its head, Stephens would procure. No questions asked.

5 October 1854

Even in this place, I am plagued by nightmares!

I dreamt last night that I was that albino python, only I was no longer trapped in the cage and I was large and hungry enough to make a meal of a man. I slithered through the back roads of London, searching for the right victim. Would it be someone sluggish I might easily overtake? Or would the better meal come from someone intoxicated, seasoned and unaware of what was happening? Or, perhaps, with my lithe body, I should consider slipping into someone's house as they slept. I could have my pick of anyone in the whole city. Man. Child. Woman...

While I pondered my evening meal, my mind wandered to Sophia. Without needing to command my body to move, I found myself at Sophia's window. A soft breeze billowed through the curtains. The window was open. Inside I slid, unseen.

I slithered across the room, to her bed. Face to face, my forked tongue licked the air, tasting her breath as it escaped from those perfect, rosy lips. Would I leave her room sated, or would her life be spared this evening? Hunger overtook me but I was unable to end a life so young and precious. I left, seeking my meal elsewhere.

While roaming once more, I thought of my captor, Mr Stephens. This man who had forcibly removed me from my happy jungle home. In a blink I found myself at his abode.

The light was on in his library when I arrived. Down the hall. Through the door. There I was, face to face with this man who had sealed my fate. He sat in a chair, smoking a pipe.

I reared up and forced him to look at me. Only I was no longer the python seeking revenge on a cruel master, I was now the cobra. Just as large as they python. I spread my hood and tasted venom drip down my own throat. Our eyes locked. I swayed to enchant him. Like looking into a fire, he could not look away from me. He was in my command. I felt the snake push me outside of myself and I watched it, spitting venom in Stephens' eyes with deadly precision. Once he was momentarily blinded – strike!

The snake lunged at the man's carotid artery. Quick, close to the surface, big. A sudden rush of venom, straight to the man's brain. The cobra looked at me. As if I could understand it, it offered to share this meal with me

I awoke. Back in my own bed. I was dripping with sweat and exhausted. After a full night of sleep, I felt as if I had been awake all night. It was not the restlessness of insomnia I was familiar with, but a new kind of exhaustion. The night had been physical and my body showed the effects.

Part of me longs to pay a call on Mr Stephens to check on his wellbeing, but today is the day we take our leave of London and travel to Paris. A delay in our departure would have a chain effect – delaying my finding Madam DuPont's sister, delaying my voyage to Andalusia to check on the wellbeing of my sister, and above all, delaying my return to England to be reunited with my beloved Grace.

A dream is all it was.

8 October 1854

I am not going to go so far as to say that the current feeling of melancholy which has overtaken me is regret, but it is definitely something akin to it. It is the beginning seeds of this emotion. The uncertainty of choice which may become the memory of the moment when a pivotal decision was made which affected one's life for the worse.

Here I am in Paris and I find myself wondering if I should abandon everything, I have been working toward for the past six months and begin my life anew. In London I am an anomaly. Foreign. Dark. Here in Paris I am more at home. I feel like after all of my wanderings I may have finally found a home. And yet, it lacks one thing which my heart yearns for above all else – Grace.

Our return to London is not scheduled for many weeks. Had our visit been abbreviated, this city would have had no chance to seduce me. Yet I fear that by the time our sojourn ends, I will be completely enamoured and powerless to resist her charms. How many times in one's life does a person stand at a crossroads and see them so clearly?

9 October 1854

The address Madam DuPont provided for her sister was, as we both suspected, no longer valid. Happily, this has not been a substantial barrier in finding this woman, Claire DuLac.

I made my first and only enquiry into her whereabouts in a bar near her last known address and the waitress nearly laughed in my face. "The Claire DuLac?" I assumed it must be "the" Claire DuLac, and answered in the affirmative. As fate would have it, Madam DuPont's sister is an actress with some reputation in the city. Her newest show is scheduled few days from now. I have already made arrangements that Wilkinson and I attend. A poor physician may not be able to gain entrée to an actress' dressing room after the show, but a Lord with Wilkinson's substantial connections and influence most certainly would.

At the theatre I saw a rendering of the woman. There was some family resemblance to Madam DuPont, but it was also obvious from where her jealousy stemmed. Claire was younger, softer and more vibrant. They shared the same porcelain skin, yet where Madam DuPont wore it like an armour, on Claire it was luminescent, lovely, intoxicating. I longed meet her just like every other man in Paris surely did, to be close to one of the most ravishing creatures on earth.

11 October 1854

Wilkinson received a letter from London today. It contained the following clipping from the Gazette:

The body of Mr Dominic Stephens was found this morning by a grocer making a weekly delivery. The police discovered several cages on the property, containing various snakes, lizards and other exotic non-native species. Cause of death is still to be determined.

Stephens' body was discovered the same day Wilkinson and I departed for France! I cannot help but wonder if my dream was some kind of psychic premonition. I would write to the police and tell them that they are searching for a cobra, but why would they believe me? Because I saw it in a vision? It is more than mere coincidence that I dreamed of this man's death the same night he died.

12 October 1854

Wilkinson and I were out walking this afternoon when we saw a blind beggar in the street. We did not give him any alms, a decision of which I am never certain, but Wilkinson did speak to him as we passed. "You're lucky that, at least, you can hear."

When taking the distilled liquid drug, my vision, my hearing, all of my senses were heightened. I was to such a degree that now, back to my normal state, I feel some kinship with this blind man. I have seen, and now am blind. I have heard, and now am deaf. And yet, according to Wilkinson's logic, I should consider myself lucky that I am not completely blind and deaf. I am lucky to have these piddling abilities, even though it is within my grasp to see for miles and hear a heartbeat through a solid brick wall.

Is a man with one arm to consider himself lucky that he still has one and did not lose them both? What a strange use of the word "lucky." Lucky to be bad off, because it is possible for things to be worse.

I am alive, now I must make the best of it. The rich man is luckier than the poor man because he has access to things which the poor man cannot fathom. But the poor man only knows this if the rich man tells him what he lacks.

I should tell Wilkinson how lucky he is that he can see, for I know how poorly he truly sees, how poorly all men see, and I know how to change it. It is not luck. Science. Magic. A mix of both, perhaps. Would this blind man be able to see again if I gave him my elixir?

14 October 1854

I have not checked the clock, but I have no doubt that it has made a full rotation and passed midnight, bringing on a new day. It must have made this journey while Wilkinson and I were still at the theatre. No doubt. No doubt.

I am overcome once more with the delirium of a man who desperately needs that sweet embrace of oblivion which can be elusive at times: sleep.

My day was spent mixing the stimulating agent so that I would be prepared for my hoped encounter with Claire. I debated whether I should take it early in the day so that its effects would be wearing off as I met her, or if I should wait to take it just prior to attending the show, so that it would still be fresh with me. My inability to sleep now makes me wish I had taken it much earlier.

There is nothing lucky in being blind. There is nothing lucky in being deaf. There is nothing lucky in lacking things another man has.

The show. The show! Claire gives limited performances, building her reputation as much by the actual show as by its scarcity. After having seen tonight's performance, I understand her reasons. Just like her sister's performances in Japan, overexposure must be avoided. There is no way to ensure a man will not buy a ticket and return each night. The only way to ensure that adequate time passes between performances is to intentionally delay the next show.

Having taken my stimulating agent, I was the only one in the crowd who experienced the real show. Everyone else was quickly overcome by the misty air, just as those hapless souls who wander into Madam DuPont's are. There were women trolling the audience, smiling. They had perfunctory jobs to perform – taking hats, selling cigarettes, ushering people to their seats – but their real job was to smile and to distribute that drug which would lull the audience into a blissful stupor.

The opening performance was spectacular. It was the only one Claire expected anyone to remember, so she made sure it was impressive. Beautiful chorus girls, dancers, acrobats, music, movement. And Claire singing sweetly to the audience.

After that first number, the spectacle diminished significantly. No more acrobats, no more dancers, no more chorus girls. Just Claire alone with a piano player, singing in a voice which, once forced to stand on its own without the full support of a chorus, was thin and wiry. She had some range, she sang on pitch, but it was not vibrant. There was no resonance. No life.

One by one, members of the audience began to disappear. I did not notice at first what was happening, where they were going – I was actually watching the show! – but then I saw those same performers from the opening, the same women who trolled through the auditorium making careful selections and escorting people from their seats. The spectators were overcome by the mist by this point, and did nothing to resist. The next morning, they would only recall that the show had been extremely satisfying and entertaining. Unlike anything they had ever experienced before.

I weighed my chances of having one of these performer approach me, and decided that it was unlikely, even as I tried to feign a stupefied gaze. I took a risk and spoke to a petit woman with her face painted stark white with bright pink lips and circles on her cheeks. Despite the mask of paint she wore, I could see the surprise and disbelief when I spoke to her, amazement that I was able to put thoughts together. This worked to my advantage, and my request that Wilkinson and I might see Claire after the show was granted.

The show did not last long. It must be one of the briefest stage productions ever mounted! The audience didn't mind or notice. After the curtain fell, they remained in their seats, quietly enjoying the effects of the drug. Wilkinson himself was overcome by the drug, which was just as well. I wanted to have a private conversation with Claire and I could have that private conversation with Wilkinson in the same room in his current state.

It was quite a shock to see Claire up close. From our seats at the rear of the orchestra section, she appeared much like she had on her poster. Porcelain skin, true, but caked with so much powder and makeup I wondered if it would chip off like plaster if the woman ever dared to laugh. Her eyes were sunken and dark. They did not reflect light, catching it and radiating it back. Instead they drank it in and refused to share. Her hands were long and thin, with fingernails which resembled claws, pointy and sharp. They were disproportionate to her body, which was ever so tiny. I could see the top of her head, easily, even with the huge wig she wore as part of her show.

When we got to her dressing room, she was just beginning to strip away the layers of the façade. Her reaction to our arrival revealed that she was expecting the players to have brought her a victim from the audience as well. She soon discovered that I was not the sort of person for whom she was hoping.

I began talking quickly, frantically. I did not want an incident before I had pleaded my case. She smiled at me, a wicked smile, filled with intent. I explained to her that I was immune to the effects of her "smile," all the while hoping that the stimulating drug I had taken masked my lies. It had not occurred to me when I was speaking with Madam DuPont that these creatures might be able to gauge the speed of my pulse just by listening, and therefore could tell when I was nervous and possibly lying. In fact, it had not occurred to me until I was face to face with Claire that these beings could live in the same state the elixir elicited in me. That they were stronger, faster and outside of human limitations. The stimulating agent caused my pulse to race quickly at all times, nerves doubtless had little additional effect. I focused a portion of my efforts on maintaining my own calm, on the off chance that my pulse could go any faster and betray me.

I saw no reason to hold my tongue in front of Wilkinson, confident that whatever was discussed would go unnoticed in his current condition. "Your sister told me how to find you," said I, hoping that by starting with the worst news first, I might be able to gain some quick advantage in the discourse. "I have none," she replied. "I assure you, she feels the same," I said. I could see that Claire's anger and confusion were being eclipsed by that one emotion all women (no matter their particular physiology) are slaves to: curiosity. Claire offered me a seat and had one of the dancers bring in a cup of tea for me, and we had a most pleasant conversation.

My words flowed freely, much to my relief. I told Claire of my research and how I believed her special venom could have tremendous benefits to mankind. A little research was all that was needed, and for that, I required a regular supply. The distance to Japan made journeys there prohibitive, but jaunts to Paris to replenish my supplies would be manageable.

My proposal was initially met with laughter. Claire expressed great concern that I would not be able to discover the secrets of the venom without dire consequences to my own wellbeing, but ultimately she lacked any genuine concern over me.

I did not hesitate to offer up Wilkinson to her whims, and then I offered myself. "A drop for a drop" was the bargain I proposed. My precious life fluids for her mysterious one. At first, she threatened to have Wilkinson and I removed, barred from the theatre, or even killed. "I have taken precautions," I cautioned. "If any harm comes to my companion or myself, your show will be exposed for what it is. Your secrets (as best as I know them) will be revealed." She doubted I could undo her, but dared not risk it. She conceded that an even trade seemed impossible. Blood was available in far greater supply. I assured her that I was not concerned which of her merry band of performers filled her part of the trade. This seemed to be the condition which helped cinch the deal and our bargain was struck. I left the room and prepared my jars while she had her fill of Wilkinson.

One of the acrobats returned to the room with me once Wilkinson had been sufficiently drained, and I showed Claire how easy the milking was. She had three performers summoned, and they filled my little jars, but Claire refused to fill one herself. The performers left and Claire sank her teeth into my neck, just as I imagined the cobra had attacked Stephens. Several minutes later our transaction was completed.

I packed up my bag and helped support Wilkinson, still in a blissful stupor, back to our accommodations.

Here I find myself, back in my room, unable to sleep. Unable to slip into that state of being blissfully unaware of the passage of time so that I might awaken, renewed, ready to take on another day. Perhaps sleep will be upon me soon.

14 October 1854 (later)

The wee hours of the morning, although not filled with sleep, were still haunted by dreams. Fantastic hallucinations more vivid than any dream, which linger in my mind still. Even now I wonder if I stayed within the confines of these walls, or if I allowed my crazed, sleep-deprived mind to will my body to wander through the streets of Paris.

I imagined that Claire appeared at the foot of my bed, forming from a fine mist. She moved to my side as if floating on air, her footfalls causing no rustling of her dress, no movement in her hair. At my bedside, she spoke to me. Tender words. Loving words. Knowing that I was not experiencing a true event, I returned her words and pulled her into my bed. After a time, we both dressed and she disappeared, once again as if turning into a fine mist. Only this time, I was carried along with her. Together, in non-corporeal form, we drifted together through the streets of Paris. We searched for someone from whom she might drink.

A stranger, unfamiliar with the city, I could only think of that blind man. Without any conscious effort, we found ourselves standing above this poor soul as he slept in the street.

Claire asked me why this was who I should choose for her. Did I not think she deserved someone wealthy? Of good breeding? A king? I responded, or at least I think I did, that these people could attend her show. She might have a politician in her audience on any given night. It was this man, and people like him, who she would not encounter on her own. He was not living. He was more than blind. No, this was the man she should visit. He needed that brief moment of pleasure to help see him through one of these forgettable nights.

The blind man was quickly aware of our presence, and held out his hand, asking for a favour. Even at this late hour, he did not sleep. Or perhaps he did, but so lightly that he awoke at the slightest noise and instantly assumed his beggar's posture. Claire knelt beside him and took his hand. She spoke softly to him, so quietly that I could not hear her words. And then she smiled her wicked, venomous smile. A smile was wasted on this man, but the effect would be the same.

To my horror, though, there in that deserted night street, Claire did not simply find the man's vein and sip. I expected her to turn his hand and take his wrist into her mouth. But no. She was once again enveloped by a thick mist, and upon its clearing where she had been a wolf took her place. The wolf looked at me, as if I should understand its mind, and then it turned toward the beggar. With a vicious growl, the wolf set upon the man and ripped him apart in a violent, bloody display. I wanted to look away, but a part of me thrilled at the sight of this primitive act. I wanted the man to get up and run – not so he could get away and therefore his life might be spared, but so I could witness the chase. So that I could chase after them. Adrenaline coursed through my body; my hairs stood on end.

But the man could not run. I was certain he wanted to. Being blind and exhausted by the hour, uncertain how the kind words of a woman had turned into a beast attacking him in darkness, he would not have known which way to run. In a moment the ordeal ended. His body rent, lifeless, the mist once again formed and as it cleared, there Claire stood. She straightened the hem on her skirt and took my arm. She smiled at me, only this time it was not the same intoxicating smile of victim and prey, but a smile of satisfaction.

I was roused from the hallucination by the sounds of a wagon rolling down the street past the window to my room. Drenched in sweat, I dressed and ran out into the streets. I dreaded the thought of finding the bloody body of the beggar littering the streets near the theatre, but I needed to set my mind at ease that the events of the night were not realized. What a strange comfort – that lunatic ravings should be preferred to supernatural events.

The streets of Paris seemed endless. I was Theseus running through the labyrinth, unsure at each turn if I would encounter the Minotaur, ready to engage in mortal battle. I had visions of the cobra attacking Stephens. I was unsure of what was real and what was imagined.

With great relief, I found the blind beggar. He hovered on the edge between dreams and the waking world and opened his sightless eyes to gaze blankly upon me as I approached. Overcome with guilt at my own thoughts, I gave the man enough money to spend a week off the streets.

On the way back to our lodging, I stopped at a boulangerie and bought some food. This was an act designed to remove any suspicious thoughts from Wilkinson's mind should he be awake when I returned. Which he was. Wilkinson and I sat together and made our plan for the day.

My services in France were not officially required, as Wilkinson had business there regularly. He had his girls, chosen and tried. This morning he did engage my services to give said girls checkups which meant a tour of some questionable regions of the city. To my relief, the girls were in fairly good health, and I did not have to give them prolonged examinations. My business in France concluded, I set off for Spain tomorrow. Wilkinson will remain in France until the beginning of December, giving me ample time to ease my mind that Isabel is well.

CHAPTER 7 - FAMILY

15 October 1854

I have done something out of character for this trip – booked an expensive fare. I have a private train compartment so that I might have some time to steel myself prior to visiting with my parents. Normally I would be happy to have the company of strangers but at the moment, I desperately long for solitude.

16 October 1854

Why do I spend so much time depriving myself of the elixir? Wilkinson experiences the pleasure of it at every opportunity, and yet when confronted with it, I take my stimulant so I am immune to the wondrous effects. With the gentle rolling motion of the train, and the private room I booked, I thought I would finally catch up on some much-needed sleep. Try as I did, it would not come. After hours of listening to rain and rails, looking out the window to the blur of nature moving past as blazing speeds, I did the unthinkable.

With a newly replenished supply in my bag, taunting me, I found my willpower and reason unable to win out over my desire for time to cease and at least one day of my brief journey to be forgotten in bliss.

I perused my samples, and decided to take the rarest one I had – that of Madam DuPont herself.

Drop upon drop, I drained nearly half the phial before feeling any effects from the substance. I had not intended to waste this much of my supply in such an idle pursuit, but there was no putting it back once I had ingested it.

I locked the door to my room, pulled the curtains tight to block all light, and allowed myself to relax. The miles rolled by and before I could clear my head enough to realize where I was, we pulled in to the station at Barcelona. I disembarked. Here I find myself, so close to home and yet I cannot yet bring myself to travel all the way there today. I have taken a room for the night.

The venom has not left me with the same feeling of contentment which I remember from before, and although I did manage to drift into another mindset for the ride here, it was not the same. I did not experience the same sense of bliss. Instead I lapsed into something more akin to a deep, sleepless rest. I imagine this is what death will be like, only from death there will be no awakening.

There is a train to Seville departing tomorrow night.

17 October 1854

The disturbance in my sleep schedule is beginning to take a toll on me. I spent a sleepless night in Barcelona. The day today, which should have been spent sightseeing and perhaps finding a small trinket or two to take to my sister, was instead spent in exhaustion.

I finally was able to sleep shortly before sunrise and fell into such a welcomed, deep sleep that the innkeeper had to force his way into my room and shake me back to life. He seemed gravely concerned that I was near death, for I had failed to respond to extended raps on the door, which eventually devolved into shouts. I was supposed to have vacated the room early that morning, and the innkeeper became increasingly concerned with each passing hour. Finally, by early afternoon, he decided it was best to investigate. I assured him that I was in good health, just tired from my traveling the day prior, and he gave me some time to collect my things, clean myself, and depart without feeling pressured. He agreed to keep my cases until that evening, for a small fee, so that I could roam the city unencumbered.

I was a spirit without substance as I walked. My mind was unsettled, as if I was sleepwalking through the city. Yet I knew I was awake. I was aware of my surroundings to some extent. I had no ambition to do anything or to go anywhere.

I continued in this condition for hours. It was only as night approached and the sun was setting that I began to once again feel alive. My mind sharpened and I remembered my plans for the day. Too late now to fulfil, I returned to the inn and collected my belongings. The point of a night train to Seville was to sleep through it and awaken at my destination. Yet here I am, awake.

19 October 1854

I have found my sister. She left Antonio only a few days prior to my arrival home and has been staying with our parents since then.

My mother is ignorant of how trying she is. Although she has welcomed me into her home, oblivious to the tension between us, to me it is palpable. I have still not fully recovered from my disturbed sleep cycle, which makes dealing with her even more difficult. My mind is clouded in the first part of the day, so her comments wash over me. To her this shows that I have mellowed and seek to mend our relationship. In truth, I am unable to respond and by the time I am fully lucid, it is not worth revisiting events from hours earlier.

There is some joyous news to record within the confines of these pages – Isabel has had her child! A boy, strong and healthy. She has told Antonio that she is only going away for a short time, to allow the baby to meet his grandparents, and to regain her strength. I could always tell when my sister was lying. She does not intend to return to her own home. Antonio's home. The move back to our parents' is permanent.

Isabel is in extremely good health for having so recently given birth. The result of the strife with Antonio was a burning desire to leave him and her body has complied by being fortified against adversity.

24 October 1854

Although my mother still sees me as a child, there is some pride in her as she escorts me around the village, bragging of my work as a doctor in London. If only she knew the true details of my current position, she would no longer feel the same.

The villagers, many of whom remember me from my youth, are pleased that I have come to visit. Long overdue, they say.

How strange, the opinions and beliefs people hold when they only see such a small part of the story. These same villagers, if they knew how my mother once disapproved of my decision to leave home and study, a lesser life choice than staying in the village and taking a wife, perhaps they would not think it was long overdue, but rather too hasty a return. This village is my mother's home, and for the first time, I feel like she could approve of me.

The days here have not been without complications but I have managed to keep my temper in check. My mother has developed several peculiar habits, perhaps as a result of a life without her children and my father sharing a home and a life, facing eternity. The house is small and my mother feels the need to constantly monitor my activities. If I stand, she asks why I have stood. If I take a step, she asks where I intend to go. If I open a door, she wonders aloud if I will go through and when she might expect me to return. I cannot so much as fetch a blanket from the closet if there is a chill in the air without having to explain myself to her. It is as if her eyes do not serve as witness to what I am doing and she needs a narrative explanation as well.

She also asks for long, detailed recounting of when Isabel and I spend any time away from her company. Isabel is much more skilled than I at telling mother enough to satisfy this curiosity while omitting the private details of what we may have done or said. For these histories, I am happy to defer to my sister.

Spending time with Isabel and her child, Cesario (named after Antonio's father), has been a treat. The days are monotonous in some ways, but the small joys of family and a child make each day new and exciting.

2 November 1854

My relationship with God, I will admit, is tenuous at best. Living on my own, I stopped going to church long ago. Here, mother has done her best to persuade me to attend mass with her and until yesterday, I have resisted. All Saints Day. A day of obligation. When I told her I had no desire to attend mass with the family, that I would be content to remain alone at home, she burst into tears and was inconsolable.

I don't understand why she is comforted more by my attending church, knowing my heart is insincere as I recite prayers, than by leaving me alone. It was only because I could see the heartache in Isabel's eyes that I relented and went with the family to church.

Of all the times to be afflicted by illness, during mass is by far one of the worst. I am still uncertain what exactly happened – an allergic reaction to the incense, perhaps? All I can recall is that shortly after we were seated, as the priest led the processional down the aisle, I began to swoon. I must have fallen into a quick sleep for I remember being in the middle of the most pleasant dream. Grace came and visited me in the form of an angel. A near blinding light shone behind her. She reached out her hand for me, and then I was awakened. It was not Grace's hand, but someone else's, shaking me by the shoulder. The world sounded as if I was under water. Someone spoke to me, but the words weren't clear and then once again, the world went black.

By the time I awoke, I found I had been moved from the church and was now in a strange bed. My skin was clammy, drenched in sweat. I fought against my fatigue and I did my best to record my symptoms and report them to anyone who might be nearby. I must have seemed insane as I spoke out. I did not know who was in the room with me, although I could tell someone was there. I could hear breathing, but if anyone moved about, or spoke to me, I was unaware. I was later told that it was my own mother who sat vigil at my bedside.

My particular ailment is hard to classify. Fatigue. Loss of consciousness. Fever. Delirium. I recall some stabbing pain in my stomach, but the memory of it has all but faded. I would attribute the illness to something I ate, but no one else from the household was similarly struck, and we have all been keeping the same diet.

The speed with which I am recovering leads me back to my original thought, that I must have had an adverse reaction to something. The logic of this – that I could be allergic to the incense, or that there could have been an ancient dust in the place to which I am particularly susceptible, or that I encountered some insect as we journeyed to the building which stung me and infected me with a toxin – escapes my mother. She sees it as a sign from God that I was struck down in his house. Her heathen son, being punished for his disbelief. If there is a God watching over us, striking me down for being reluctant to attend a mass, only going to humour my mother, makes him seem like a cruel God I do not wish to know further.

It could also have been psychological. Perhaps my body was rebelling for me when my will had been too weak. I allowed my sympathetic nature to get the better of me by being in that building in the first place. If I had stood my ground, remained at home, despite my mother's pleas, perhaps I would not have had this episode. Perhaps I would not have encountered whatever it was that triggered this. Or, just as possible, perhaps I would have had the same attack while I was here, alone. My family would have returned from church and found me in a near-death state, collapsed to the ground, and been overcome with panic. At least in the church, they had the comfort of friends to help keep sound heads and attend to me when I was in need.

Already, one day later, I am nearly recovered. I am confident that by this same time tomorrow I will feel as fit as before any of this unpleasantness happened. I will forget this, but I know my mother will not. Ah, just one more reason I am glad to be leaving here soon.

12 November 1854

The past three days seem like such a blur. A bad dream which, perhaps, still consumes me. I find myself on a train bound for Paris, my visit with my family cut short by some weeks.

I imagine I allowed myself to believe that the situation with my mother and sister was more idyllic than it truly was. Isabel was there because she had left her husband. I took for granted that he would be complacent in this. I do not consider myself someone so innocent as to accept that people will react peacefully when confronted thus, and yet, I found myself doing just that. How would I feel if my wife left me with our newborn child and never intended to return? No matter how strained our relationship had become, this would be a terrible blow.

And so it was that when Antonio realized Isabel was not returning to him, he sought her out. He arrived at our parents' house early in the morning when the whole family was out at church – aside from myself who had sworn off attending mass after "the incident." The incident thankfully was enough to convince my mother that it was in all of our best interest for her heathen son to stay home. God did not want me in church, and I did not want to be there.

If God's hand had any influence, I must assume God wanted me to greet Antonio. I fear it was not God's doing, though, which influence the events.

Antonio knew my parents, so it caught him by surprise to find me alone in the house. We had never met. I, on the other hand, had no idea who this angry man was who, without uttering any pleasantries, began to demand where my sister was. Caution overtook me, and I gave vague answers to all the questions he spat at me. Isabel was out. I did not know when she would return. I am her brother.

I could see the rage, the betrayal, in his eyes. I invited him into the house to wait. I invented a pretext and I slipped into my room. I sent immediately to my elixir. The liquid extract. I desperately needed to warn my sister and parents off from coming home, but if I left on foot at a normal, human pace, Antonio would be suspicious of my actions and be able to follow me. I saw no other option than to improve my own physical condition to gain an advantage and ensure the safety of my loved ones. And yet I hesitated, wondering if this was the right way. Was this the only way? They would be home soon. I didn't have time to consider other options. I had one option before me and I needed to take it. I drank.

Antonio made me feel like a child in comparison. He had a height advantage of several inches. And he has spent his life toiling so that his muscles are well-worn where mine are soft. Spending my time hunched over a work bench lighting fires under test tubes has not prepared me for fisticuffs. I am not so foolish or filled with pride to hold any illusions that I might be a physical match for this man. No, I had little choice but to drink.

My pulse was already racing, beating rapidly from the moment Antonio had arrived and not slowing down its pace despite my efforts to maintain a calm demeanour. I returned to the family room in my parents' small house where I had asked Antonio to wait, and I secretly waited for the drug to take hold. I tried to play the calm, hospitable brother-in-law, acting ignorant to Antonio's rage. I told him I had recently arrived from London and was staying for a short time, and that my family had not told me the details of how my sister had come to be there. The distrust in his eyes revealed that he knew or at least strongly suspected I was lying. I now realize it was foolish of me to pretend to not know intimate details of Isabel's life considering Antonio was aware of how frequently we corresponded. He knew we were confidantes.

The conversation with him was stilted. He did not travel there to be friendly and visit with family. He was a man on a mission – to retrieve his wife and child. As we sat in a moment of uncomfortable silence followed by uncomfortable silence, I wondered what exactly my plan was. I needed an excuse to slip away without arousing suspicion. Or, would I just leave knowing he would not be able to follow?

As soon as the drug took effect, I made my decision. I told Antonio I was supposed to have a meal prepared for the family when they returned from church and he would need to excuse me while I set to work. Since he had no interest in me particularly, he gave no protest as I left him unattended and retired to the kitchen. I made a show of preparing a meal, going out to the garden several times to fetch various ingredients. Antonio did not watch me. Instead he kept his focus tuned to the front door. He would stand and move to the window, peeking outside. He would even open the door a crack to watch the road should anyone be arriving.

I went to the garden once more to feign picking herbs and off I ran. I stayed away from the road, sprinting through gardens and leaping effortlessly over walls. I gave little thought to being seen since I knew most of the villagers would be in church. I practically flew to the church, arriving just as mass ended.

I slowed my pace and did my best to appear nonchalant as I approached the church, hoping to casually encounter my family just as they were making their egress. As I approached the building, I began to feel ill. I thought back on my previous visit, and realized that with my metabolism heightened, whatever it was on the premises which affected me thusly, I was even more susceptible to it now. Where before I was able to sit in the church for some time without having a reaction, now, with senses heightened, I was still more than fifty feet off when I began to swoon. I quickly turned and made my way down the road, stopping under a shady tree to compose myself.

Once I had gained some distance from the church, I felt recovered and waited for my family. They exited the church soon enough. The next several moments seemed an eternity to me. Members of the congregation insisted on visiting with my sister. "Oh, what a charming baby!" "It has been ages since we've talked." "How is your son doing?" I was nearly unable to bear it one more moment when my family turned to the road and began the walk home.

I watched my father as they drew near, realizing that despite my mother's wishes, he would not be able to continue this weekly ritual much longer. Perhaps even as soon as in a week's time, he would be too feeble for this walk. Riding a horse would be no better, and although he could ride in a coach, without someone younger and more fit to prepare and steer the thing, he would be homebound. Would my mother give him a special dispensation?

Needless to say, my family was surprised to see me. I told them that Antonio had arrived, with fire in his eyes, and that I thought it would be best that they not return to the house. I assured them that I could entertain Antonio until boredom got the better of him. But Isabel – dear, headstrong Isabel! – insisted that they return home and confront him. She firmly believed that if she ran again, her whole life, and Cesario's, would be spent running. She did not want to live a fearful life.

I admire her courage, but time can make a man forget his rage. My council was that she should allow time to work its magic on Antonio, lessening his memory and his rage, and confront him at another time, when the wounds of her leaving were not so fresh.

Although my parents and sister did not believe that I would get home much sooner than they, I insisted that they let me leave them and return to Antonio, lest he realize I was absent.

I did my best to contain myself until I was well out of sight of the church crowd, then took off running at full speed. I was back in the kitchen in moments. Antonio was just where I left him – looking out the front window. To make sure he wasn't suspicious, I went in to the living room and offered him something to drink. He declined, slightly startled that I had approached so quietly. I returned to the kitchen, only this time I really did prepare a meal for the family.

It was not long before I heard my family returning. I went back into the living room where Antonio looked out the front window. I asked if there was any sign of them yet, and he did not answer. I knew they were near, and I headed for the door. Antonio physically stopped me from opening the door, insisting that he wanted his arrival to be a surprise. His hand gripping my wrist, I contemplated the rage within him and decided it was too soon to play my hand. Better to allow him to intimidate me away from the door than have a physical confrontation with him now.

As soon as the door opened, Antonio lunged. But it was my mother he lunged at. On instinct, I sprang into action, restraining the man. For the first time he could feel how powerful I was. There was a palpable shift of control. He became complacent as I helped him sit down on a chair. Isabel and the baby then came inside. I stayed an arm's length away from Antonio, told my mother that food was ready in the kitchen if she wanted to go set the table for us, and I suggested to Antonio that perhaps he should talk his problems through with my sister.

I felt like an intruder, but I was not convinced that Isabel would be safe if I left her alone with him. Isabel did not hold anything back, airing every grievance she had had with Antonio since the day they met. Some of her complaints came as a surprise to Antonio and seemed frivolous to us both. By the end of it, it really did seem like progress had been made. However, Isabel did not tell Antonio she had no plans of returning to him. She argued that she needed time away from him, and that soon she would be back to her old self. Antonio assumed that meant she would come back to him, but both Isabel and I knew she was thinking of herself prior to the one Antonio knew. Not her old self, but her true self. Isabel's true self was not someone who would be content being contained by Antonio. To be fair, she would not be content being contained by any man.

Antonio's temper cooled, though, and our parents invited him to stay in the house for a few days before returning home. With how hospitable everyone turned, I wondered if I had made a mistake in taking the drug.

I was able to easily excuse myself from eating at the luncheon, explaining that I had done a fair amount of sampling the food as I prepared it. My mother began to show serious concern when I also declined to dine in the evening and she noted how lethargic I was all afternoon. As night fell, I began to feel alive and as soon as I was certain the household was asleep, I set off.

Without shoes, I ran through the fields, gardens and empty streets of the village. How different this place was than the other cities I had been in on my night-time prowling. In the English countryside, there were no people. It was all animals. Wilderness. The tame wilderness of England and the quiet estates of the wealthy. In London there was humanity. Activity. It didn't matter what time of night you went out, you could find someone else unable to sleep who you could engage in conversation to help pass the waning hours. Here it was different still. The streets were deserted. Not as crowded with buildings as in London, but in the heart of the village there was a fair concentration of them. But by this hour they were all deserted. The properties were smaller, closer together than the vast grounds of Wilkinson and his neighbours. Here you actually had an awareness that you had neighbours.

The village is largely self-sustaining, so there are many functioning gardens and even the poorest person will have a small stable, coop or pen in their yard to keep some livestock. I must have visited the property of every resident in town, and I did not find a single human awake.

Although I was alone, the run was exhilarating. This is the part of the drug I so desperately missed. The freedom, the strength, the power. The night world belongs to me and I defy anyone to come and try to take it from me!

I thought of Grace. My heart raced even faster. What a delicate dance we are engaged in! How would she react if she saw me now? Running barefoot through the night. Leaping up to high tree branches and throwing myself into the air as if I could fly? I behaved like a child running down a hill on the first warm day of summer, and felt just as pleased. If Grace were here, I would hoist her up onto my shoulders and carry her through my world, showing her the wondrous secrets only I could see in the dark. How funny that just thinking about her could make my heart race so.

I never tired. I felt no hunger or thirst. I did not sweat or feel flushed despite the physical exertion. I just felt alive! Too quickly I began to notice subtle changes in the light and a new crop of animals emerging from their dens, signalling that dawn was near. I had no choice but to return home and resume the charade of being myself.

My mind reluctantly returned to the house and though I was still a considerable distance away, I heard Cesario crying. A few paces nearer and I heard that not only was Cesario crying, but there was another stream of noise underneath – Antonio and Isabel arguing.

I ran to the house in the blink of an eye and I found a hiding place outside where I could listen to their conversation. The argument was heated, but they did their best to keep their voices down, allowing Cesario's crying to drown out their own voices to the average ear. Once Cesario had been calmed, Isabel forced the conversation to an end, promising Antonio they could resume later in the day, in private. Although I had missed the beginning, I had heard enough. Antonio spoke to my sister disrespectfully. There was no love in his voice, only anger. Antonio returned to bed and Isabel sat up with Cesario for a while.

I snuck back into the house and decided to leave my sister this time alone with her child. The sun was brightening the world, and soon the whole house would be awake. I needed to pretend that I had spent a similar night to the others, embraced by slumber.

The next day was filled with tension, but we all tried to pretend that everything was fine. Antonio's true nature became more difficult for him to control with each passing hour. He started by whispering insults to Isabel he thought no one else could hear, and by the time the sun fell, he and Isabel erupted into screams. My poor, distraught mother could not calm either of them. All she could do was hold Cesario and try to comfort him.

I stayed near, as protection. I know Isabel would have preferred privacy, but she could tell by the look in my eyes that there was no way I was going to leave her alone with this man. And then, as their argument became most loud and heated, Antonio reached back and threw a fist at Isabel's face. I intercepted it with such speed that I'm sure neither he nor Isabel could recollect how it all happened. As I stood there, holding his wrist, inches away from my sister's face, I began to feel some of the rage I saw in his eyes. I could rip his arm off, I thought to myself, or worse. It was only because Isabel spoke, urging me to release him, that I did not do any real harm. A bruised wrist would serve as a reminder that Antonio should not raise a hand in anger again if I was in the room.

Although I wanted Antonio to leave immediately, my kind parents refused to put him out at such a late hour. They instead encouraged him in the idea that leaving the next morning would be best.

Antonio and Isabel's fighting during the day had provided ample distraction to keep my mother's attention off of me and the weird habits I was forced to exhibit because of my current state. My mother showed no concern that she had not seen me eat that day, because our meals were irregular. When I told her I had eaten when she was outside playing with her grandson, she believed me.

How much of the drug had I taken? In my passion, I failed to measure it out properly and as a result I could not estimate how long the effects would last. One thing I did know, once it wore off, I would fall into that deathly sleep for days. I needed to warn my parents lest they think I was seriously ill. Having already had one mysterious illness in the church, I was already formulating my story on what the illness was, why I was afflicted, how they were safe, and what they should expect from it.

That night I once again felt a surge of energy and took to nature.

Long before sunrise and my predetermined time to return "home," I decided to head back that way. When I got there, Isabel and Antonio were fighting once again. This time my parents were awake, cowering in their bed, pretending not to hear.

Rather than remain a voyeur this night, I walked into the house through the kitchen, and encountered the lovers as they fought. Antonio stank of alcohol, and although perhaps he did have a buried memory of the power of my hand, he was too intoxicated to call it forward. Antonio swung his fist and I easily dodged. He continued to swat at me, looking the fool as I easily evaded his every move. Although I should have been more tolerant of this poor, helpless fool, I felt rage building in me unlike I have ever felt before. As Antonio shouted insulting things about my sister, I did not feel contented to let the exchange continue this way. I felt it was my duty to fight back.

I took one swipe at him, not even at full force, and in an instant he was on the ground. It was then that I looked over at Isabel and saw a look of horror on her face. As upset as she was at her husband's behaviour, this was the first time she had ever seen me act the brute, and it is something I know she will never forget. Our relationship changed forever in that moment. Seeing her brought me out of my rage and I retired to my room, leaving Antonio in a heap on the floor.

I heard him stagger to his feet and storm out of the house. As soon as I reached my room, I was overcome with fatigue and fell to the bed. Perhaps my body had known the elixir was wearing off, and that was why I had returned so early this night. Regardless of the reason, I worried that I would not be able to protect my sister if I fell in to the deep sleep I had before, which could last several days. Not only had I shown her a brutal side of myself, but now I would not be able to protect her.

In my dreams I was once again visited by an animal. Now it was the wolf who I had seen in Paris. It came to me and led me outside. Once outside, the crepuscular beast showed me how to track Antonio and together we ran through the fields until we found him. I stood aside as the wolf howled into the night, and his pack appeared. They set upon Antonio, tearing his limbs apart. Eating his flesh and drinking his blood.

Then I was standing not in a field, but in my parent's own front yard, Isabel standing at the door. From the look of terror on her face, I knew instantly this was no longer a dream. I saw Antonio's bloodied body, torn apart, lying on the ground before me. I tried to explain to her that the wolves had done this thing, but before I finished, she spoke. "There were no wolves. You. I saw you. You did this thing." Despite my protests that this was not possible, that despite whatever rage and, and, and venom she had seen in my eyes only a short time before, I was still the same man she knew and loved and this was not something of which I was capable. It was dark. She just couldn't see the wolves.

I could see in her eyes an expression I had never before seen. She was not afraid that I would hurt her, but she had the look of a protective mother. I was unpredictable, and she could not have that around her child.

We went back inside and Isabel set about packing my things. I tried to protest, but she would not allow me to stay. The damage to Antonio's body was extensive. No man would believe it had been done by anything other than a wild beast. Isabel wanted me to leave. As the good brother, I agreed. Our parents were awakened by the sounds of us arguing and they came in. I told them that I suddenly remembered I had promised Wilkinson I would return to Paris by the fourteenth, and I apologized for letting the days get away from me. Isabel decided to remain quiet about Antonio, only saying that they had had an argument and he had gone out for a walk to clear his head.

My parents tried to convince me that I should stay until the morning, but a glance at Isabel told me that I should leave right away. The only hope I had of preserving our relationship was to do as she wished now, and hope that time would ease her worries.

And so I find myself back aboard a train. At times I feel like my life is spent in transit. I started to feel like Spain was my home once again... It was the right time to leave. I have spent hours trying to recall the exact events of that night, but each time it is the same. There was no blood on my clothes. No blood on my skin. I was a bystander at this brutal act and that is all. Not a participant. My only comfort is that Isabel and Cesario will be better off for the loss.

CHAPTER 8 - LONDON

15 November 1854

Wilkinson is still in Paris. Not wishing to resume my subservient role to him just yet, I have taken a room in the deuxième arrondissement, away from the river. I made anonymous inquiries to ensure he was in residence in the same lodging as when I left, and will join him in a few days. Until then, I need to take some time to return to my normal state of health.

Most of the drug has left my system, and yet I did not fall into the deep stupor as before. I slept on the train during the day traveling here, but each night I was alert, as if awakening from a good-night's sleep. My schedule has somehow been shifted. I need to get it back in accordance with the rest of the world. At night I wander the streets out of boredom. I have grown weary of spending nights awake in a dark bedroom. I find getting out into the world, although stimulating, to be a better pastime. I become drowsy just as dawn approaches, falling dead away in the morning hours.

I have not resumed a regular dining schedule yet. Some small ulcers are forming on the roof of my mouth, which make eating any solid foods an unpleasant task. I have been drinking hot beverages, tea, and worry that I will lose a significant amount of weight if I am not able to eat a regular meal soon.

Being in Paris, in a big, vibrant city, also has hindered my ability to resume a regular schedule. There are many places a man can go in the night to find other kindred souls. Those who find the night more suited than the day for living. I wake up and head to the theatre, then go to those places where people congregate after hours. Together we pass the time.

With winter upon us, the days are growing shorter. The sun is only up for nine hours. I am trying to work myself gradually back to a normal schedule, staying up into the morning. later each day. I wait to leave my bed and enter the world until later each night, but the temptation of the city by night is alluring.

18 November 1854

I have not been able to manage staying awake on my own, so today I decided to resort to external means. I have taken the stimulating agent to ensure I do not fall asleep during the day. While roaming the city, I stumbled upon a small apothecary where I found some valerian root. I will take it this evening to help settle my nerves and ease me to sleep. I cannot rely on my own willpower. I have already managed to stay awake well past noontime. Even if I am not able to effectively return to my normal pattern, I will at least be able to resume working for Wilkinson without causing alarm.

19 November 1854

I managed to stay awake today with less of the stimulant than yesterday. However, I was still very tired throughout the day. I did not have much energy to leave my room. As the sun set, my energy swelled, which I took as my cue to ingest my herbal remedy to induce slumber.

While waiting for the root to take hold, I decided to pull out my paper and pencil and draw a picture of the view from my window. Although Isabel has decided to have me be away from her and Cesario for now, I have resolved to continue to be a part of his life through my letters and drawings. I hope that Isabel's love for me has not faded away so completely that she would not share a letter with her child or that she would not continue to write to me.

The strange thing was that there were sketches in my pad which I did not remember drawing. Disturbing images from my dreams. The cobra striking at Mr Stephens. The wolf standing over the beggar in the street. Sophia asleep in her bed. I studied the drawings. I could not deny that these were drawn in my own style, in my own hand, yet I had no recollection of creating them.

23 November 1854

One drug to wake me up in the morning. One drug to help me sleep at night. Another drug tempting me from within my satchel. How can something so innocuous, something without emotion or meaning, without life or will, be such a powerful force that it consumes my thoughts so completely?

I should destroy the whole supply. I did not travel with all of it, but destroy what I have here and when I return to London, have the strength to destroy all that I left behind. But I cannot. There is value in it. Beyond my own use of it, it is important. It just needs proper study.

I take the phial out of my case nearly every night. I turn it around in my hands. Feel the weight of it. Watch the liquid fall around the edges. The liquid clings to the glass, as if the glass also does not want to let go of it. It is only by eventually leaving my room that I am able to put it away and free myself from the temptation of it. Once I leave this place and return to a more normal life, a regular schedule in Wilkinson's household, I think I shall have an easier time resisting. Now it is difficult because my life has no regulation. I force myself awake, I force myself asleep, inflicting an arbitrary schedule which in Paris I do not need to abide. It is only for the benefit of my return to London that I put myself through this. And what happens when I return to London? Will I sit idly by as Grace and David marry?

25 November 1854

I sought Wilkinson today in anticipation of spending a few final days in Paris before returning to London. Much to my surprise, Wilkinson's own condition has deteriorated in my absence. He has become completely obsessed with Claire DuLac and her troupe, visiting every performance he can. When the theatre was dark, he would spend his days loitering in the area, hoping to encounter Claire by chance, or at least so that he could make it seem like chance. Yet she never leaves the theatre.

Fortunately, the same day I decided to rekindle our relationship, Wilkinson received a letter from his wife urging him to return to London. Grace, it seems, is having second thoughts about the wedding. She has revealed to her mother that her heart has been tempted by someone other than David (my heart leapt at the thought that it might be me!) and that perhaps she was hasty in agreeing to marry him. Rather than humour her daughter, Lady Wilkinson has decided it will be best to set the date of the wedding for this winter, December 31, so Grace's worries can be put to rest through marriage. She requires Wilkinson to return home to help her with the preparations and to help her convince Grace to go through with the wedding and not do something rash.

Now I must be the voice of reason. How ironic! If Wilkinson knew of my own private struggle, I doubt he would be so willing to consider me wise council. Yet his own condition mimics my own in many ways -- bouts of insomnia, lack of appetite – and as his consulting physician I am have been able to convince him that it is for his own health that we must return to London immediately, never revealing my own private desires.

Arrangements are in place for us to leave tomorrow. Wilkinson wishes to spend one last night in the alleyway behind the theatre. I cannot risk that tonight will be the night that Claire DuLac decides to finally leave her den, and so have decided that, although I may not be able to convince him to have a full meal with me, I will convince Wilkinson to share a drink with me and his will be laced with valerian root as well. We will both sleep a drug induced slumber this night and I pray that one of us will be able to awaken in the morning and set us back on course.

I am confident that once Wilkinson is away from the influence of this unholy woman, he will return to his normal state of health quickly. Within a matter of days. My own prognosis is not so cheerful.

27 November 1854

As much as I felt a sense of returning home when traveling to Spain, it is doubled whenever I return to London after a long absence. This truly is my new home. My true home. Or at least it has become so.

Lady Wilkinson has done wonders with the house. When we left, it was musty and curtained. It felt as if we were staying in an abandoned building rather than a home. But now it is warm and welcoming. Full of life. Not only because of the unpacking and cleaning up, but because now it really is full of life, full of people. A home this large was not meant to be lived in by one or two people. It is meant to bustle with activity. Children running around the halls upstairs. The cook toiling over a hot stove in the kitchen. Smells of a wondrous meal wafting up to the rafters.

Wilkinson and I arrived at the house just after supper, and were both secretly grateful to be able to make our excuses for not wanting anything to eat prior to retiring for the night. I informed Lady Wilkinson that her husband was having some insignificant illness and that he would need plenty of rest for a few days prior to being thrown in to the full responsibility of the wedding preparations. Not two full days away from Paris, and Wilkinson was nearly fully recovered. I sit here and wonder when the same will happen for me. We should both be weary after our long journey, and yet once again, with night full upon us, I feel more awake and alert than a sparrow singing in the morning.

Grace has been sequestered in her room by her mother. Lady Wilkinson forbade her from having any visitors other than her own immediate family and fiancé. I can only hope that with her father's return, the restrictions will be lifted. I long to see her.

28 November 1854

How long has it been since I've looked in a mirror? It doesn't seem like something I would intentionally avoid, and I have not, but with my focus diverted to my own health concerns, I have taken little notice of my appearance. I'm sure there were mirrors and windows in Spain and Paris where I caught my own reflection, but I haven't really looked back at it, until this morning.

How different I look. Not that you wouldn't recognize me, but somehow I just did not quite look like myself. I feared that having fasted so much of late I was wasting away to nothing – perhaps subconsciously this was one of my reasons for not looking – but that is not the case. I was quite surprised to see that, despite my feelings to the contrary, I appeared quite well. My skin has lightened considerably as a result of my new, preferred schedule. Even when taking my drug to be awake and alert in the morning, I found myself not wanting to leave my room until very late in the day. I have seen so little of the sun of late, and my skin reflects this. I am pale. But my body looks fit, my face only slightly more angular than I remember. Perhaps it is for the best if I have lost some weight.

Wilkinson is recovering. He is able to awaken in the morning and join the household without my assistance, and I suspect that this evening he will fall into a deep sleep unaided.

The more remarkable event of the day, though, is that I have been asked to examine Grace tomorrow to ensure that it is not a physical ailment which is causing the uncertainty in her betrothal. Now I face my own dilemma. Do I enter her chamber as I am and allow fate to have her way, or do I do something rash, which could condemn me to a lifetime of uncertainty?

I firmly believe it is too soon to expose myself to any component of the elixir, no matter how diluted it may be. My body has not metabolized the last dose, and may never.

29 November 1854

I visited Grace in the early afternoon, her mother escorting me to her room and threatening to sit just outside, listening. I am fairly certain that it was only a threat and that she did not actually monitor our visit. As soon as I saw Grace, I felt myself beam. I don't recall smiling so much since first being reunited with my dear sister, which now seems like a lifetime ago.

The visit began formally. I played the part of doctor, giving Grace a physical examination to ensure that she was not suffering from some obvious ailment. No bump on the head. No fever or aches. But we both felt excitement ripple through our bodies as we touched, I know it. The door closed, she pulled me close to her and whispered in my ear that I was the one who had so swayed her heart and my own heart leapt to hear these words!

We needed to formulate a plan quickly. Her mother would soon return and ask me about my findings. If I determined that Grace was well, she would continue to be sequestered and I would be denied future access. My only option was to declare that Grace was suffering from some minor ailment which would need some regular treatment.

Lady Wilkinson did return quickly, making her own determination of how long our examination should take. So eager was she that her daughter should marry this other man, that when I told her I would need to embark on a radical treatment with Grace which would take several hours each day for a week or more, she believed me instantly.

I longed to pull Grace into my arms and kiss her and cling to her, but I only nodded and left. I went roaming the streets in the afternoon to find innocuous medical supplies which I could bring back for my "treatment," which would look convincingly severe in their operation. I also visited Eugene.

30 November 1854

What a glorious deception Grace and I perpetrated today! I set up my equipment very near the door and it could not have performed better. It sputtered and smoked, sending the occasional spark under the door and a good deal of fog. It also made such a din that, although somewhat annoying, Grace and I were able to converse without needing to be overly concerned that someone's prying ears might be pressed up to the other side of the door, listening to our every word. Any ears pressed to the door would only hear the equipment hard at work.

I told Lady Wilkinson to leave us for two hours, but she insisted that whatever treatment I was giving to her daughter should be completed in one hour. Although she does trust me, she is not overly trustful. Or perhaps she fears I am conspiring with Grace, giving her an alibi while she sneaks out of the window to meet with her lover. One hour would not be enough time for Grace to sneak out and successfully return, but two hours might afford her that privilege.

I cannot now recall the details of our conversation. I promised that I would bring my sketchpad the next day and draw her. I remember my emotion, which I hope Grace shared. This feeling of not wanting time to pass. It did not matter if we spoke – words had no meaning. I was greedy for time, wanting it to stop so that I could look upon my love for all eternity. If I had all eternity to gaze upon her face, I know I would never tire of it.

I pressed my hand into hers and squeezed her so tightly I could see for a moment it became uncomfortable for her – yet she did not ask me to lessen my grip. Feeling our flesh held together, I wanted to squeeze her so hard that our hands should join and we would become one.

All too soon our hour was over, signalled by a light knock on the door. I quickly mussed Grace's hair to make it look like we had been engaged in some active treatment, and sat her by the machine. Only once I was satisfied that our charade was in place did I open the door to her mother.

Lady Wilkinson examined the machine, which I then turned off, our treatment ended for the day.

1 December 1854

Through all of my journeys, it appears I have picked up a new skill. I have never thought of myself as being a particularly good orator, and yet my tongue does appear to have picked up some silver of late. I can only attribute this to my frequent travels, during which I have found myself in new and unusual situations where talking was a valuable tool. I had not noticed this until today.

Grace and I had a marvellous session. I took my sketchpad with me and drew the most incredible drawings of her! My muse! My hand has never been so confident. It was almost as if it was guided by God and I merely pushed it across the page. I drew quickly and the drawings were so lifelike, so perfect. I showed them to Grace and she nearly wept at seeing them, never imagining I had such a gift.

When I left her room, Lady Wilkinson met me in the hallway to get an update on Grace's condition. I assured her that Grace was recovering her senses as quickly as could be expected, and very cordially reminded her that longer sessions would see faster results. She hesitated, but I felt particularly charming for some reason and pressed the issue. Before I knew it, she not only agreed that longer sessions were in Grace's best interest, but she also seemed to think it was somehow her own idea! As I spoke, so she repeated what I said, nearly unaware that I had put the words directly into her mouth.

In the late afternoon I decided to pay a visit to Felicity, bolstered by how well my meeting with Lady Wilkinson had been. Although it took some convincing to get Felicity to open the door, once she did and we were face to face, her demeanour changed. I have not seen her as rational in a very long time. We sat for over an hour, talking about what troubled her. She was calm, though, and when she came to a break in her thought, I was actually able to offer my opinion without being quickly interrupted by the usual endless stream of consciousness jabbering. Once again, I spoke and she repeated the words as if they were her own. Not everyone who is alive is plotting to steal from her. Some people are genuine and want nothing from her. She needs to be more open to trusting people. As the sun began to set, I got up to leave and she seemed genuinely disappointed to see me go. She invited me to return soon, and I promised that I would.

2 December 1854

With our visits extended, Grace and I finally allowed ourselves to succumb to passion. If allowed to continue for all eternity, I would still need more time with Grace. But I must exhibit restraint until Grace and I have fully plotted our future together in a way which will not completely destroy her familial relationships. Her family is very important to her, and I must respect that. Her happiness is of the utmost importance. My own desires have been deepening with time, and now with my prize so close, I cannot afford any missteps which will alienate my love.

I heard the floorboard creak, an alert to Lady Wilkinson making her way down the hall to lightly rap on the door, letting us know our time together was at an end for the day. We said hasty farewells and declared our desire to see each other again. How funny we treat time. Cursing it for going too fast, pleading with it to speed up other times. We are never content to let time pass at its own pace, always believing we know better.

When I went downstairs with Lady Wilkinson, I was greeted by an unpleasant surprise – David had returned.

He insisted on discussing Grace's condition with me. He desperately wanted to see her, but he did not want to do anything which would jeopardize her recovery. He had resolved to accept my wise counsel on when it would be best to visit with her, vowing to leave once more if seeing him now would set Grace back.

What an opportunity was presented before me! The temptation to continue lying to everyone was great. I could send David away until right before the wedding, by which time Grace and I would have already made our plans and have left this place.

And yet I did not deny him. I want my relationship with Grace to be pure. I do not want to forever wonder what motivated Grace. I have enough guilt over using the elixir to catch her eye in the first place, now that I have it, I want to know that her heart really belongs to me. That she has committed fully of her own free will, and that it is not merely the result of isolation and confusion.

How strange that I allow myself to become complacent in such a short period of time. In only a matter of days I nearly forgot all of my troubles. I forgot that David would return. I deluded myself into thinking that somehow the wedding would be stopped without any active participation from either me or Grace. And I have not done any experimentation on the elixir since my return.

I have not felt any temptation in days to even look upon the bottles. They flew out of my head! I only think upon them now as David has returned and I am experiencing some primitive territorial desire to protect Grace as if she were my property. I instantly thought of using the elixir as a way to increase my strength and vitality so that I could engage David in a physical confrontation, driving him away from this place.

But instead I have decided to allow Grace to make her choice. Whoever she chooses, I will accept her decision.

3 December 1854

David spent several hours with Grace last evening. Lady Wilkinson allowed him to bring her supper and they dined together. I was tempted to linger in the hall to try to overhear their conversation, but propriety forbade me. Instead I retired to my room early and stewed in darkness.

How fickle I am. Not in my devotion to Grace – that is unwavering. No, I am fickle in my willingness to lie, cheat and steal to make her mine. Capricious. At times I am overcome with an intense desire for our relationship should be untainted by deception. And at other times I believe any means at my disposal which can help me win her heart is fair and should be utilized. What an arsenal I have at my disposal, to not only thrill Grace's emotions, but to also disable my opponent in this battle. The question of whether I should use these weapons plagues me.

I rely heavily on sleeping aids in the evening and stimulating drugs in the mornings to keep up the appearance of normality. Yet last night, for some reason, the sleep aid did not work. Long, sleepless nights do not benefit me. By being confined to my room, lights dimmed, I am forced to pass the time with my own thoughts pounding like thunder in my brain. Only a few days ago, if even that long, I was content to let things progress as they were. Now that David has returned, perhaps my time has expired. To know the secrets of that woman's heart! If I only had some indication of Grace's true desire, I could find some comfort. But even if I were to ask her, how would I know her words were true? How can we ever know what is true? We cannot know another person's mind, their heart, their soul. No matter how well we think we know them, it is only that self they wish to present to the world that we know.

And what if knowing Grace's mind did not bring the comfort I seek? There is no guarantee that her heart belongs to me. It is only my desire that it should be thus. How ironic it would be to eventually discover that David and I were actually both pawns in Grace's own game. Helpless players and she orchestrating each move only for her own amusement. It is quite possible that she loves neither of us. Perhaps she is only seeking a convenient way to escape from underneath her father's thumb and whichever of us proves to be the more effective means of that escape will win the love she proffers.

I have nothing to offer her. I am from a humble family. I have no money, no property. I am little more than a servant in this household. Will she entrust her future with someone who cannot guarantee the secure life her mother seeks for her? David's prospects are brighter. Even if he does not make his own name, his family name is worth more than I will earn in ten lifetimes.

17 November 1854

Querido Diego,

I have started this letter many times since you left, but each time I reach a point where I cannot continue. Perhaps this time I will succeed.

What can I say about Antonio's death? No one suspects that his injuries were inflicted by a human. How could they? I have not been able to stop thinking about the sight for any measurable length of time. Each time I close my eyes, I see him. Each night as I sleep, I see you standing over him.

I worry that you are possessed, my brother. I know you have severed your relationship with God, but to see how you swooned in church and the animal look in your eyes that night, I can think of few other explanations. I have not been able to discuss this with our parents. I know that Mother would instantly attach herself to the idea and the rest of our living days would be spent praying for the salvation of your soul. All I can ask is that you seek some spiritual guidance and know that you will be in my prayers. I hope that in time I will be able to look at you and see the brother I once knew. I suspect there will always be some lingering fear when I look at you, and it pains me to say this to you.

You have always been my heart. Like another part of me. And now, I feel like you are a stranger.

Please allow me some time to think about what I have seen in you. To learn how to accept it if it is truly the person you have become. I do not want you out of my life, certainly not in such an abrupt way, but for now I need some time and I hope you can grant me it.

If you are wondering, yes, you may write to me. But do not take offence if I do not answer. There is so much going on with Antonio's death, telling Valentina and now raising Cesario on my own, that simply reorganizing my life will take much of my energy. When I came to stay with our parents, I did not know if it was going to be for only a few days or longer. Now one thing is certain, I will be staying at home for much longer than I had ever imagined.

Know that I am praying for you.

All my love,

Isabel

5 December 1854

Isabel's letter troubled me all day. That she is so profoundly worried about me is troublesome. Does she see something in me which I myself am blind to?

Some days it feels like the world is conspiring against you. Not only did Isabel's letter arrive yesterday, but I was also denied my time with Grace. Lady Wilkinson insisted that missing one day of treatment would not be detrimental. Before I was able to wake myself, she had removed Grace from the house. She took her out to make some arrangements for the wedding. Meeting with the seamstress, going to the flower market, visiting friends in the city. It was a cold day, but clear, and likely to be one of the best to come for a while, so Lady Wilkinson seized the opportunity to tend to her errands with Grace at her side.

By the time they returned, I had already received the letter from Isabel and was in a sullen mood. Had I pressed, perhaps I would have been able to spend a short amount of time with Grace in the early evening, but I worried that my mood would be unwelcomed and I decided it was best that we miss this one day rather than force our companionship. God willing, there will be many more days for us to spend together and this one lost will scarcely be missed.

I felt inclined toward solitude and skipped supper, instead deciding to retire early. I took an extra dose of the valerian root, hopeful that I would drift away quickly and sleep long through the night. I dreaded one more night turning restless in my bed until just before sunrise when sleep finally opens her arms, welcoming me in. The weed took hold quickly, but my sleeping was plagued with vivid dreams. This morning I worry that just as that night in Andalusia when Isabel woke me from my daze that perhaps my dreams last night were also a blend of reality and hallucination which my tired mind could not work out. Do I now, this morning possess any proof that I remained confined in my chamber last night and that I did not roam these halls? It is only because of the fantastical things I saw and experienced that I believe the events of last night were a dream. I know my mind has lost some ability to realize what it is truly experiencing.

I waited in my dream for the sounds of the household to quiet and then I began to roam. I visited my Grace's room. I did not disturb her in her sleep, lest in her excitement she cry out and alert her parents to my presence. Yet shortly after I arrived in her room she began to stir and I worried that I would be caught. There was not time for me to get back out of the room if she were to open her eyes at that moment, and surely she would be startled.

Then I heard a voice in the darkness. "I am with you." I kept my eyes trained on Grace to see if the voice had disturbed her. I was holding my own breath so that the only sound I made was the beating of my own heart. Since I did not answer the voice, it spoke again. "Do not worry." My anger growing that this unseen presence in the room would bring Grace out of her restless sleep, I allowed myself to whisper back, hoping to keep my own voice quiet enough that it would not travel the length of Grace's bed. "If you insist on speaking, you insist on waking her." "Let her wake! I am with you," the voice responded.

"That she should wake and see me in her chamber would be fright enough, and require many countless hours of explanation to her parents, but your voice is unfamiliar to me and therefore I have no question that you are a stranger to Grace as well."

"I am a stranger to Grace, but if she were to awaken, she would see what we want her to see – her chamber empty. I am with you and therefore it is as if you are not here."

I could not contain my curiosity further and I allowed my eyes to wander the room. It was not until I had turned my head very far to the side that I saw it. A chameleon was perched upon my own shoulder. In my dream, I dismissed this. It was not worrisome to me. I have travelled with snakes and wolves, a chameleon seemed almost natural. I spoke again. "Show yourself, stranger!" There was harshness in my voice, although I spoke in hushed tones.

"You have just cast your eyes upon me," he replied. I looked back at the traveller on my shoulder and he nodded his head.

"You yourself have told my story, so do you doubt that I will make you invisible before your sleeping love's eyes?"

I remembered the story of the chameleon I had heard in Africa and passed along to my dearest sister. "I have done you no favour that you should decide to sit upon my shoulder."

"I sit where I please. You will give me shelter, I will give you my ability of disguise in payment. If you wish your words to be heard, they will be heard. If you wish yourself to be seen, you will be seen. I do as you desire."

Grace came very close to waking up at this time, so I decided it would be best that my conversation, no matter how veiled, continue someplace more private where, should this beast on my shoulder be less than honourable, we would not be discovered. I have no recollection of leaving the room. I did not lift a foot to take a step nor did I raise my hand to open a door, and yet I no longer stood at Grace's bed, watching her. I was back in my own room. I lit a lamp and sat down on the bed. The chameleon climbed off of my shoulder and stared at me.

"Must you touch me for your power to work?" I asked. Although it was unlikely someone would come to my room in the wee hours of the morning, I was nervous as the chameleon looked at me that I was now very much exposed. With the creature on my shoulder, I was shrouded in darkness. Now, I felt as though the sun shone directly on me alone.

"At first. But I will teach you. You will learn quickly and you will not need me."

"And then where will you go?"

"I am here now, that is all that matters. I do not worry about what will happen to me tomorrow. My only concern is where I am now. What am I doing now? Is it a good place to be? Am I happy? I will react to this immediate situation and change myself if the situation changes."

"What has looking to the future gotten you so far?" the chameleon asked.

"It guides my whole life. All of my decisions. I am where I am because I keep one eye on the future."

"By keeping one eye on the future, you have become a slave?"

"I am a free man. I do as I please. I live in London, far from the rural village where I grew up. I am a success."

"You work for a man you hate. You spend your days pining over a woman who is unavailable, betrothed to another and due to wed any day now. You allow her to distract you from your research – the only thing which was giving you any real happiness. You keep secrets. You lie. You are estranged from your sister, who you adore, who you thought adored you. You sleep all day and roam the corridors of this house alone by night, still keeping one eye on the future hoping that the next night your condition will be improved. And yet, it is not. For all your looking to the future, you are firmly planted where you are. You cannot progress if you only try to make grand leaps instead of putting one foot down after the other and moving with a determined stride."

"How long have you sat on my shoulder, chameleon, that you have such an intimate knowledge of my life?"

"Long enough to see that you need me," the chameleon answered. I began to consider what the chameleon had said. Is this how I imagined my life would be? Grace's wedding was only a few weeks away and here I was, holding out hope that she would call it off and run away with me. What did I have to offer? I was a slave, her father's slave, with no immediate means to support her without Wilkinson's support. No, no, I stopped myself. Thinking of all of the potential outcomes again, this is what the chameleon told me I did. If I do this, then this will happen and I'll be happy. Only it didn't work that way. I would do my part, but the world never complies. And in doing my part I found no pleasure.

How far behind was I on my research of the elixir? If I had not spent my afternoons with Grace or plotting how to spend more time with her, would I have unlocked its secrets by now?

Those moments between the dream world and the real world blended together until I found myself lying in bed, staring at the ceiling. Was I awake at last? Had I ever been asleep? I could not shake the thought that despite my love for Grace, she was an obstacle to my truly excelling in my research. Would we ever be happy? Would her father allow us to be together or would Grace forever resent me for separating her from the family she so loves?

My own family... If Grace were to insist that I would never see them again, I would comply. It is only through some misplaced sense of obligation that I maintain any ties with them. Aside from Isabel. And what if Grace were to become jealous of the love I feel for my sister and refuse me to see her again? An impossible choice and yet this is what Grace most certainly faces if I press her to continue our relationship. Her parents approve of David and he will make her happy. Maybe not at first, but in time. A life with me will wither. Happy at first, miserable at last.

7 December 1854

The wedding preparations continue. Several members of Lady Wilkinson's family have come to the house to stay and help. No longer is this the deserted, lifeless house it was when I first came here, furniture covered in sheets and whole rooms sealed off. Dust so thick your shoes not only left a trail where you walked, but also needed to be polished daily to keep the dust from settling. Now there was life everywhere. Giggles ringing down the hall as the women tied ribbons and arranged flowers. The men gathered nightly by the fire to commiserate over how foolish the women were with the plans.

And where does this poor physician go in the middle of all this bustle? I wish we were back in the country so I could retire to my private little house and stay out of the whole situation. Here I am, not servant exactly, and certainly not family. The men stop talking when I enter the room, shooting steely glances my way. I am not forbidden from staying, but I am certainly not invited to join. And the women have no warm reception in them for any men at the moment. Unless I decide to reveal to them my hidden skills with a needle and thread, they have no use for me. The giggles stop as soon as they hear masculine steps approach.

I am but a ghost. Wilkinson has no use for me at the moment, aside from caring for Grace. Why I make any effort to regulate my schedule is a mystery even to myself. If I were to sleep all day, it would not be noticed. Despite my best efforts and heaviest drugs, I am unable to find more than a few hours sleep each night just as the sun threatens to return to the sky.

Is this how I pictured my life would be? No home. No wife. No practice. The adventure I was promised by Wilkinson kept me entertained for a time, but now it is over and who knows when another voyage will occur. Until such a time, I am his extra servant with no specific skills. I do not cook. I do not clean. I could serve as his translator if he had international business dealings in France or Spain. He sees me as less than equal. Another man he owns. I do not sit with him and the men and engage in their conversation. I do not sit with the women and make ribbon decorations. My only companion is the cook and she has little time for an idle man in her kitchen.

8 December 1854

The chameleon visited me again last night. I wonder if it was a dream at all! I was only just about to take my valerian and pray for sleep when I felt those wild eyes staring at me. I turned my head, and there the creature was, sitting upon my shoulder. "Do you really want to sleep tonight?" the chameleon asked.

"I want to sleep most nights," I answered.

"This house is full of life. Let us go look at it, together. I'll protect you."

What interest had I in watching Wilkinson's family sleep?

It was almost as if the chameleon could read my thoughts, sensing a shift in my attitude and a willingness to go out with him. "Good. We'll leave the house. Tonight, I will give you your first real lesson."

We stood outside in a part of London I had never been to before. "How did we get here?" I asked.

"Thought moves your spirit. I suggested we spy on the members of your household, and your thoughts brought us to this place."

"Man cannot travel on the power of his thoughts."

"No. Man cannot."

I heard a footstep and hid in the shadow of the building. "Do I need to hide?"

"Yes and no. It is certainly easier to go unseen if you hide, but if you really want whoever is approaching to take no notice of you, if you hide or not is of little consequence."

The man (I knew it was a man long before I could see his face) came closer still and before he had rounded the corner and come into my field of view, I realized who this man was. It was David I had come to see. My rival. But why? Did I want to spy on him? Did I doubt his loyalty to Grace? No, he was alone and I knew he was returning to his family home from seeing Grace.

Confrontation then. Here is this man who is the barrier to my happiness. Now it was time to ask my second question of the chameleon. "Where are we?" I laughed at the thought of it – me asking a reptile questions in a dream. I decided I was dreaming and that my actions therefore would have no consequence.

"Far from the Wilkinson's home. It has taken David a fair time to make his way home, although we travelled it in only a few seconds."

"I thought our travel was instant," I interrupted.

"Seemingly so, but no. Your thoughts led you here, your body needed to travel through space. But be assured we are a long distance from where you are thought to be, and no one will ever suspect you could have travelled here once the facts are collected tomorrow morning."

"The wolf and the snake," I started when the chameleon interrupted. "They will be here if you summon them," he answered.

I stayed in the shadow and watched as David walked down the street, coming nearer and finally passing me. He didn't see me standing there even though the shadow did little to conceal me in truth. As he walked away, I saw the cobra slither behind him. "No!" I shouted out. David didn't turn. He didn't hear me, but the snake was called off and I found myself once again in my room.

The chameleon crawled off of my shoulder and up onto the wall and disappeared into it.

9 December 1854

I overheard Wilkinson talking with an associate today about America and the business opportunities available to entrepreneurs. Perhaps I should travel to America, leave all this behind and start over again. What a dark cloud has settled over my head! I watch Grace in the throes of her wedding preparations and see her genuinely happy. Although she may love me passionately, she is giddy with delight at choosing silks and laces, flowers and ribbons.

Is she the kind of woman who will be happy assuming her place beside a man like David? Playing mother and hostess with no desire to pursue her own interests? Needlepoint to keep her hands busy during the idle, long days and no ambition beyond the front door? Is this the woman I fell in love with?

My own Nomadic spirit is pulling me away from London already, although I have not yet determined where I shall go. I've been here long enough and my life has stagnated.

I'm so completely exhausted. Energy feeds energy. Stagnation...is exhausting. I wanted to wake up with the sun, with the rest of the world, and participate. Now I wonder why I ever bothered. What is there for me during the day? A few stolen hours with Grace which may or may not come? Being treated like a second-class citizen by Wilkinson and his friends? Is there value in this existence for me?

If Grace were to choose me over David and her family were to consent, what then? Would Wilkinson treat me as an equal, as his son, or would I be a second choice, ruining his daughter's life? It would be a façade. Perhaps I would continue to work for Wilkinson, or perhaps I would resume my practice. Find a new place, make contact with Mary and Thomas to try to help them with their concerns. Try to help Felicity find peace of mind and pray that in her insanity she does nothing to harm my own family. Is that what I should set out for myself as a life goal?

I adore Grace so much that mere words cannot express how I feel and yet...

And yet I wonder if our lives are truly meant to overlap or if our time together is already coming to an end.

The chameleon questioned this very part of human nature. Why do I spend my sleepless nights with my mind troubled by these questions instead of trusting my instinct and acting on it in the moment? But if I did that, would David now be dead?

My human nature is the very thing which separates me from these creatures I fantasize about. Without my worries about the consequences of my actions, I would be no better than those wolves which tore Antonio apart. And yet are they to be judged harshly if their motive in attacking him was hunger? It worked out for the best for all; the wolves were fed and an evil man faced justice.

Grace is not yet mine and already I feel her like a weight, a chain confining me to this place, to these people. A life with her is a life of misery. I cannot be the man she needs and she cannot be the woman I desire. Love...

Is not enough.

10 December 1854

I am so tired of being tired. If I find the courage to follow through on my plans to break free from my current situation, I will embrace my body's will and sleep all day and roam the streets at night. There is plenty of activity in London by night to keep me entertained, and if it means no longer being in this constant battle to regulate my schedule, the better off I will be.

I worry that I have not been thinking rationally for some time because of these disruptions. Is it possible to keep a sound mind while always being tired? Surely the mind dulls just as the other senses do from constant fatigue. In truth, Grace's wedding preparations have been a saviour to me. I have not had to do much actual work for Wilkinson in some time since he is busy with more family arriving each day. If he were free to spend more time with me, I've no doubt he would notice the toll this strain is having on me.

I need strength now.

12 December 1854

I met with Grace today and ended our dalliance. It went surprisingly well, which still confuses me.

We were able to meet for our regular medical appointment this afternoon and almost immediately once the machine was started up and creating its diversionary noises, I sat Grace down and spoke to her solemnly. I told her that I did love her deeply, but that I did not think the life I had to offer her was everything that she deserved in life. David would be able to provide her not only with the stability and wealth she was accustomed to, but his love for her rivals my own and I know he will always place her happiness first.

I thought I saw a tear begin to well up in her eye, but I leaned over close to her, clasping her hands and spoke with a smile, "It is for the best. Trust me." Her expression became blank and she recited my words back to me. I felt like she was under some spell and anything I had told her to do, she would do. I waited for more from her, but she said nothing. I held her hand for a few minutes longer, hoping somewhere deep within myself that she would stop me, but she said nothing.

I was the one who had to fight back a tear as we opened the door to the hall, Lady Wilkinson waiting there for us. I told Lady Wilkinson I thought Grace had made tremendous progress and that there was a good chance today's session would be the last one needed. We would know more in the morning, but I was optimistic that all was well.

The quantity of stimulating drugs required to awaken me in the morning has more than doubled, and I cannot remember the last time I was able to sleep except in the early morning hours just prior to sunrise. I felt particularly fatigued after my visit with Grace and decided it was best that I retire to my room. It was already late afternoon and I hoped by the time the sun set, I would feel refreshed enough from a nap that I could rejoin the household without having been noticed.

Once in my room, I pulled back the covers on my bed and was startled to see a cobra lying in wait for me. I remembered some things about the snake from my time in Africa, and immediately stepped as far back as I could. If the cobra became antagonized, it could not only strike out at me to bite, but the range of its venom is remarkable. The serpent did not take a threatening pose, instead it looked at me and I swear, if it is possible for a snake to smile, that is what this one did.

Now I must question if all of this happened after I fell asleep, otherwise I fear that sanity has started to slip away from me. It is one thing to be visited by a talking chameleon after having closed my eyes for the night, and quite another for a cobra to greet me in the middle of the day! I have convinced myself that the chameleon is the product of delirium and hazy dreams, but I have no recollection of my head hitting this pillow before this new hallucination began.

"Are you pleased?" the cobra asked. "What?" was my answer for I could think of no reason why I should be pleased to find a snake in my bed. "Did you not see me in the room with you and Grace? I helped her accept what you said and not suffer for it."

"You?" And instantly it made sense, but perhaps that is only because I so wanted to believe. I was distraught over having ending my relationship with Grace, over having given her up for her own good, and although it pained me that she was not sharing in my suffering, I was pleased that she did not have to endure it. Once I had realized what the cobra was suggesting, I also realized that I was relieved for this assistance. "Yes. Thank you."

The cobra, satisfied at having done a good job, slithered toward the edge of the bed, ready to head off into whatever otherworldly place it regularly occupied. But I stopped it. "And when I originally asked Lady Wilkinson for permission to treat Grace, were you there helping me, too?"

"I am there when you need me," the snake said. It then disappeared under the bed. I pulled back the covers and pushed aside the mattress. There was no crack, no hole where it could have gone. It seemed to have dissolved into air. I sat on the bed and after a few minutes reluctantly reclined, unable to keep my eyes open a moment longer. I knew I should be afraid knowing that this snake resided somewhere hidden in my room, but I was too exhausted to think about it.

14 December 1854

I have decided to leave this house. This much I have known for some time. There is no way for me to continue working for Wilkinson and be around Grace without going mad. Perhaps I have already gone mad.

I went out yesterday afternoon and looked at several rooms for rent around the city. Without a job, I will not be able to afford the luxury I have become accustomed to, but perhaps I will resume my private practice. Specialized. Catering to a more nocturnal clientele. One of the flats I looked at was in a dank basement. Dreary. Cold. But it did have potential if I were to resume seeing patients. It was large and cheap.

I feel like my life is ending. I am allowing myself to be defeated this way.

I started going through my possessions, preparing to move from this house, and stumbled across my forgotten experiments. A cobalt phial mocking me. How many sips would solve my problems? Turn me back into that god I was that one night when I first swayed Grace's heart in my direction? Is that the answer I have been searching for?

The rebellion my body has been staging, it is possible it is a protest that I stopped experimenting on myself with the elixir.

16 December 1854

I could not bring myself to face Wilkinson. I left his house in the middle of the night, a note pinned to his door explaining nothing more than our time together was at an end effective immediately. I do not know if he will search me out, fearful that I will reveal his secrets to powerful people in London who might undo his family in scandal. At one time I would have feared such a powerful man seeking me out with impure intentions, but my current mind state is such that if he were to summon demons from Hell to carry me down in a bath of flames, I might welcome the distraction.

I find myself in my new home, a basement with no furnishings. I took the linens from the bed with me so I might be able to make up a place to sleep on the floor, and tomorrow I will set out in search of some small comforts which might help turn this dungeon into a home.

CHAPTER 9 - NEW LIFE

3 March 1855

It has been such a long time since I have put my words on these papers.
If I were to meet the man who first started this journal, I would find him
a stranger. I no longer need to write down events to keep them fresh in
my mind. I can recount the events from yesterday, and the day before,
and the day – the month! -- before that, as if I were living them again in
vivid detail. It is solely for posterity that I felt the need to make one last
entry here.

Where to start? Grace and David had their wedding. I did not attend and
other than occasionally seeing them in the evening at an event, our lives
have completely moved apart. I still adore her and wish her well, but
keeping away from her is best for us both. How well I know that now!

I did unlock the secrets of the "elixir," at long last. Just as the venom of the cobra necrotizes the flesh, so did the elixir. It was eating away at a part of me and replacing it with some decayed rot which has now taken over. Oh, not that you could tell to look at me. I look perfectly well. More so than I have in many years. Healthy, strong. But I am no longer the same. I have been replaced by a beast. The animals who professed to be my allies were merely my own mind seeking some way to protect me from the wild urges I was suppressing. The animals are still with me, but I recognize now that they are part of me and that their actions are my actions. Perhaps one day my mind will be strong enough to let them go, but for now, they offer me comfort and explanation.

I took my final, fatal dose of the elixir just after writing my last journal entry and it was the last bit needed to fully convert me to a creature of night. Just like my poor rats, the sun is like fire on my skin. I am relegated to the nocturnal world. I still see patients, but I have another, more lucrative side business, following the cue from Madam DuPont and her sister. Strictly on appointment. I am doing very well for myself, serving London's degenerate upper-classes. Wilkinson has even come to see me professionally and begs to know how I learned the secrets to which he first introduced me. The price he pays me now makes the salary I had while more regularly employed seem like change you would hardly stoop over to pick up if you saw it in the gutter.

I left the dank basement and moved into a more well-appointed home, although due to my new skin sensitivities I still spend my days sleeping in the basement – all the windows blacked out.

Although Isabel still resists talking to me, I send money to her and Cesario regularly, along with pictures which I draw for him. I want my nephew to think my life is still filled with travel and adventure, so I draw things I encountered during my travels with Wilkinson. My memory is highly improved as is my skill at art that I can render a drawing which, if full-scale, would fool the spectator into questioning the very reality of it. I also write to Isabel's neighbour and send him money, and in exchange he does send word back on how my dear sister is. I hope, in time, she will come to forgive me, and that she and Cesario will have a more prominent place in my life.

My former patients learned I had resumed practice and have remained loyal to me. My ability to treat has never been better and I am fast gaining a reputation as the best doctor in London. Albeit one with unusual habits and a rumoured dark alternate profession. The respectable clients don't take notice of those rumours, though, so my two lives are distinct.

My animals find waiting for clients boring at times. It is lucrative, and satisfies my worldly needs, but in the wee hours of the morning, we all get restless. The wealthy aren't much fun. They don't run fast enough and are too easy to catch. No, in the early morning there is nothing like the thrill of finding a young, healthy man and giving him the chase of his life. I have yet to meet one who has proven my better, though. If they give a good fight, sometimes I'll take mercy and let them go. But the wolf is hard to control once the blood is pumping.

The nights are growing short once again. I suppose where once I was a man of summer, lazing for long days in the hot sun, now I must become a man of winter, waiting for the seemingly endless nights and basking in the shimmering moonlight.

The wolf is hungry this morning, and I think I'll oblige. We'll go down to the river to see if anyone is out and about at this hour. Where once I wondered if it was un-human of me to feel a desperation while eating, likening myself to the wild animals, now I find joy in the ability to experience the pure abandon of the wolf while hunting. I am no longer conflicted over one thing which when I first moved to London caused me some distress: Ich fresse.

The End.

CAMILLE SHARON

Camille lives in Tujunga, CA, surrounded by feral cats, some of which she allows inside her cottage. She received her MA from California State University, Northridge, in mass communication with an emphasis in screenwriting. The character of Diego first entered Camille's life while working on that degree, over 15 years ago, and he never left. When she isn't staring at her computer, tablet or phone, Camille enjoys playing piano or guitar, tap dancing, and doing all sorts of crafts.

Want to learn more about Camille Sharon? Visit her website:
www.CamilleSharon.com

A. R. MEYERING

Award-winning author A. R. Meyering is the creator of the steampunk-fantasy series The Dawn Mirror Chronicles. She is an LA native, an all-around oddball, and a self-proclaimed knight errant. Her dark fantasy novel, Unreal City, was the winner in the horror category of the Literary Classics International Book Awards. It also received a Moonbeam award and garnered positive reviews from Publishers Weekly and Readers' Favorite. She is a lover of all things historical and philosophical.

Want to learn more about A. R. Meyering? Visit her website:
www.ARMeyering.com

NOTES